THE DRAGON SLAYER
–FOLKTALES FROM LATIN AMERICA–
BY JAIME HERNANDEZ

A TOON GRAPHIC
TOON BOOKS, NEW YORK

A JUNIOR LIBRARY GUILD SELECTION

For Carsy

Editorial Direction and Book Design: FRANÇOISE MOULY

Associate Editor & Research Assistant: ALA LEE

Aztec Designs and Motifs: GENEVIEVE BORMES

Coloring: ALA LEE

JAIME HERNANDEZ'S artwork was drawn in India ink and colored digitally.

A TOON Graphic™ © 2017 Jaime Hernandez & TOON Books, an imprint of RAW Junior, LLC, 27 Greene Street, New York, NY 10013. TOON Books® and TOON Graphics™ are trademarks of RAW Junior, LLC. *The Dragon Slayer* and *Tup and the Ants* based on *Latin American Folktales: Stories from Hispanic and Indian Traditions* by John Bierhorst, Pantheon Books, © 2002 John Bierhorst. *Martina Martínez and Pérez the Mouse* © 2006 by Alma Flor Ada and F. Isabel Campoy, originally published in *Tales Our Abuelitas Told*, Atheneum Books for Young Readers. Used by permission. All rights reserved. No part of this book may be used or reproduced in any manner whatsoever without written permission except in the case of brief quotations embodied in critical articles and reviews. All our books are Smyth Sewn (the highest library-quality binding available) and printed with soy-based inks on acid-free, woodfree paper harvested from responsible sources. Printed in China by C&C Offset Printing Co., Ltd. Distributed to the trade by Consortium Book Sales and Distribution, Inc.; orders (800) 283-3572; orderentry@perseusbooks.com; www.cbsd.com. Library of Congress Cataloging-in-Publication Data available at https://lccn.loc.gov/2017042011. A Spanish edition, *La Matadragones: Cuentos de Latinoamérica*, is also available.

ISBN 978-1-943145-28-7 (hardcover English edition)
978-1-943145-29-4 (softcover English edition)
ISBN 978-1-943145-30-0 (hardcover Spanish edition)
ISBN 978-1-943145-31-7 (softcover Spanish edition)
18 19 20 21 22 23 C&C 10 9 8 7 6 5 4 3 2 1
WWW.TOON-BOOKS.COM

IMAGINATION AND TRADITION

by F. Isabel Campoy

"If you want your children to be intelligent, read them fairy tales. If you want them to be more intelligent, read them more fairy tales."
—Attributed to ALBERT EINSTEIN

ALLIGATOR

LIZARD

DEER

DOG

JAGUAR

VULTURE

Aztec & Maya Pictograms

Tales have the power to open up our imagination. From childhood to old age, our lives are framed by the stories we tell. Folktales, passed down orally through generations, show us the world by taking us through the customs, values, and cultural traditions of a people. Fairy tales may be populated by princesses, ogres, and talking animals, but they also take us into the homes of common folk solving real-life problems.

Everything that happens in the land of the popular "cuentos" or fairy tales was once invented by the pure magic of a storyteller's fertile imagination. As the stories grew and changed with every telling, the anecdotal became universal. Folktales often contain moral lessons; instead of telling us how to behave, they show us the implications of right and wrong behaviors to help us develop our social and emotional intelligence. They teach us how to be better human beings.

The Latin American heritage is richly diverse, a unique blend of Old World and New, spanning a continent across many geographic boundaries and cultures. When the Spaniards landed in the 15th century, they brought their medieval stories brimming with castles and dragons. But since Spain is itself a land at the crossroads of many cultures, these tales already contained Catholic, Jewish, Arab, and Moorish influences. The Europeans' encounter with Maya, Aztec, Inca, and other Native American cultures – themselves widespread across land and time –produced one of the most diverse and varied storytelling traditions, with a story for virtually every taste.

A recurring theme in the Latino experience is a celebration of strong women. Like so many señoras and señoritas in Hispanic families, the independent mothers, sisters, and daughters in these folktales have the inner strength to rise above obstacles and to overcome adversity. But above all, the reality of Latin American folktales is that magic can happen at any time. Listen to these stories and tell them to others: sharing these tales will ground us in our communities and give us a window into others'.

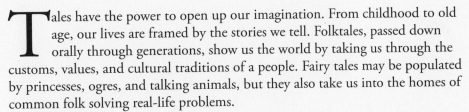

MONKEY

RABBIT

SNAKE

EAGLE

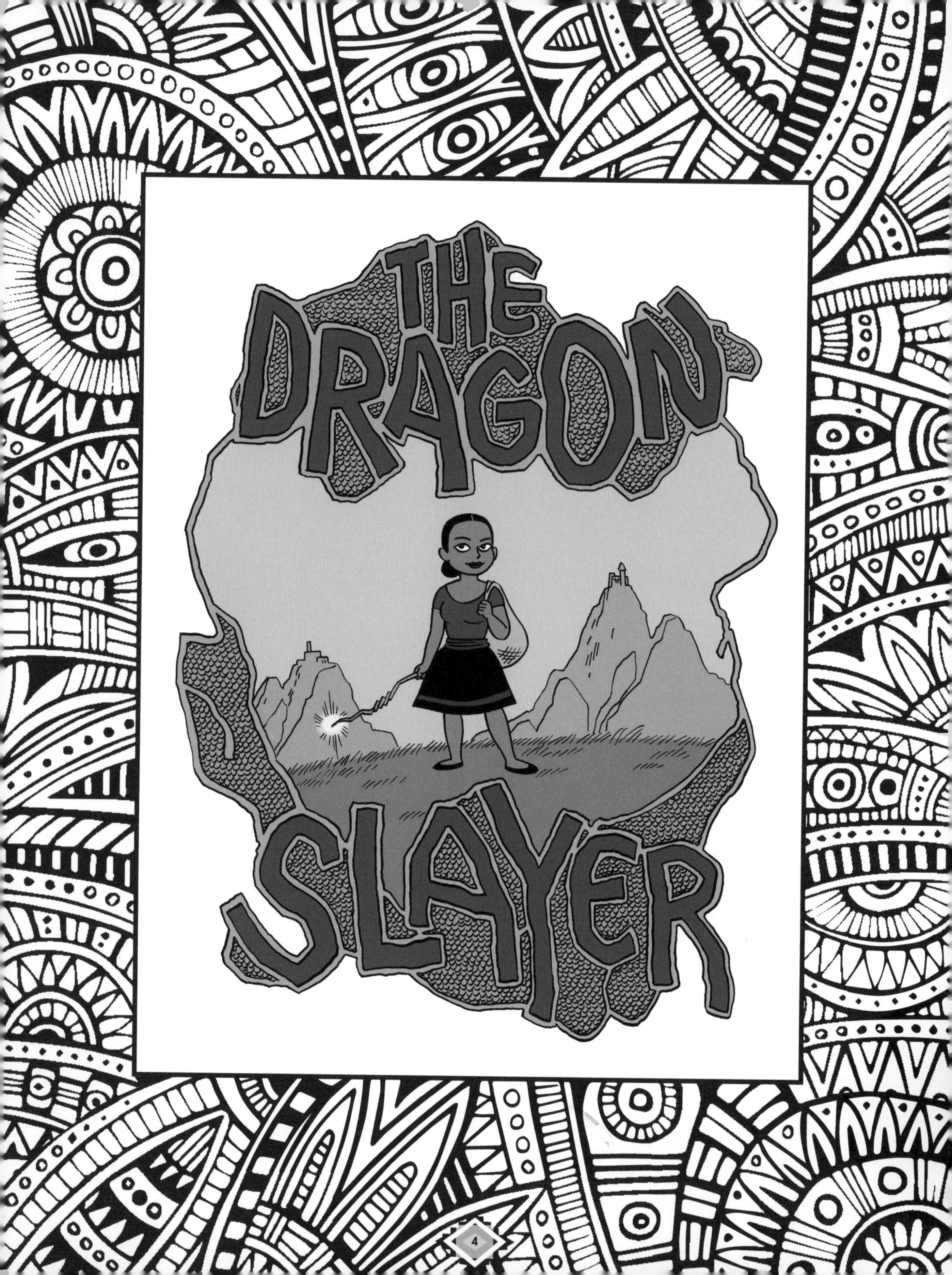
THE DRAGON SLAYER

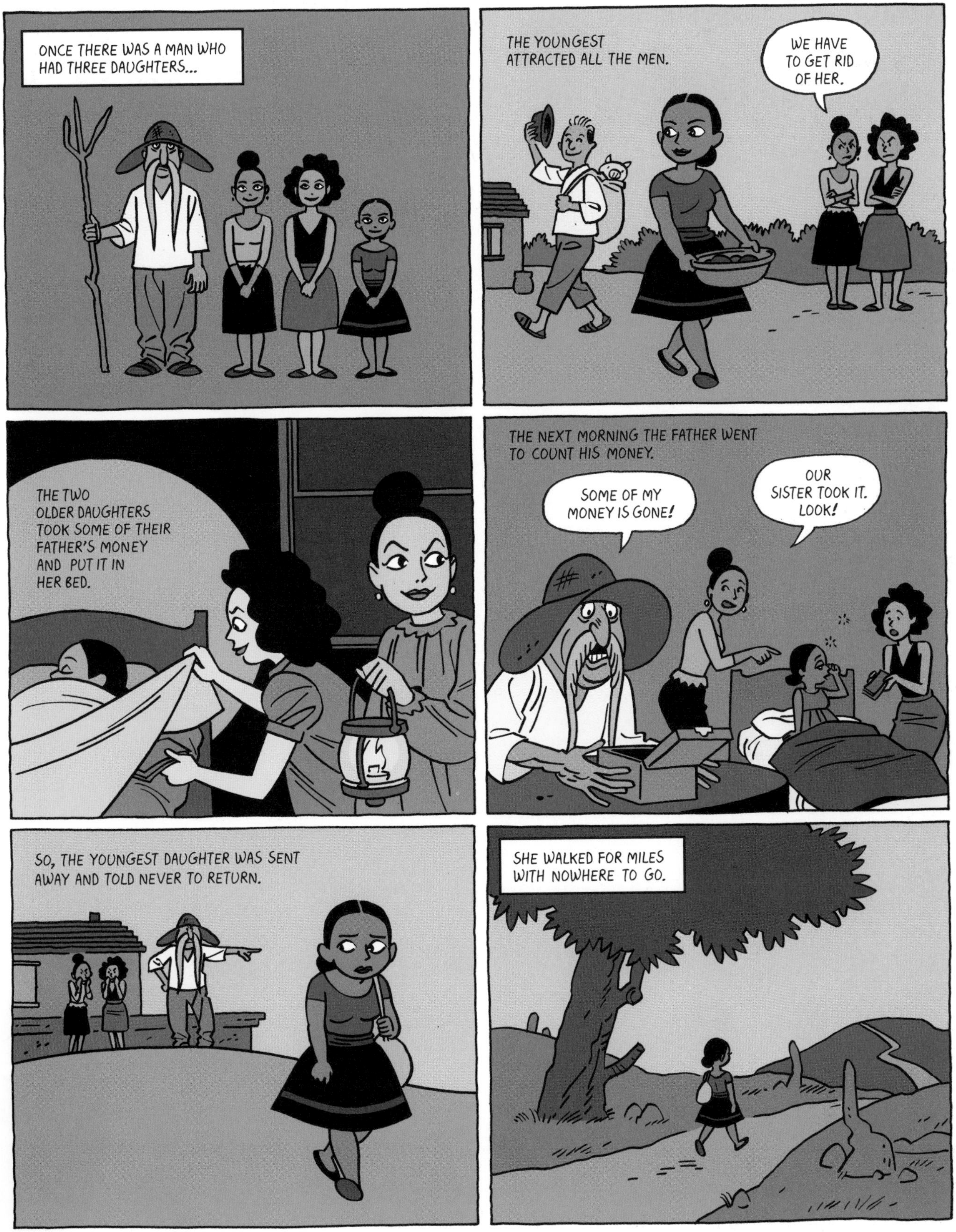
ONCE THERE WAS A MAN WHO HAD THREE DAUGHTERS...
THE YOUNGEST ATTRACTED ALL THE MEN.
WE HAVE TO GET RID OF HER.
THE TWO OLDER DAUGHTERS TOOK SOME OF THEIR FATHER'S MONEY AND PUT IT IN HER BED.
THE NEXT MORNING THE FATHER WENT TO COUNT HIS MONEY.
SOME OF MY MONEY IS GONE!
OUR SISTER TOOK IT. LOOK!
SO, THE YOUNGEST DAUGHTER WAS SENT AWAY AND TOLD NEVER TO RETURN.
SHE WALKED FOR MILES WITH NOWHERE TO GO.

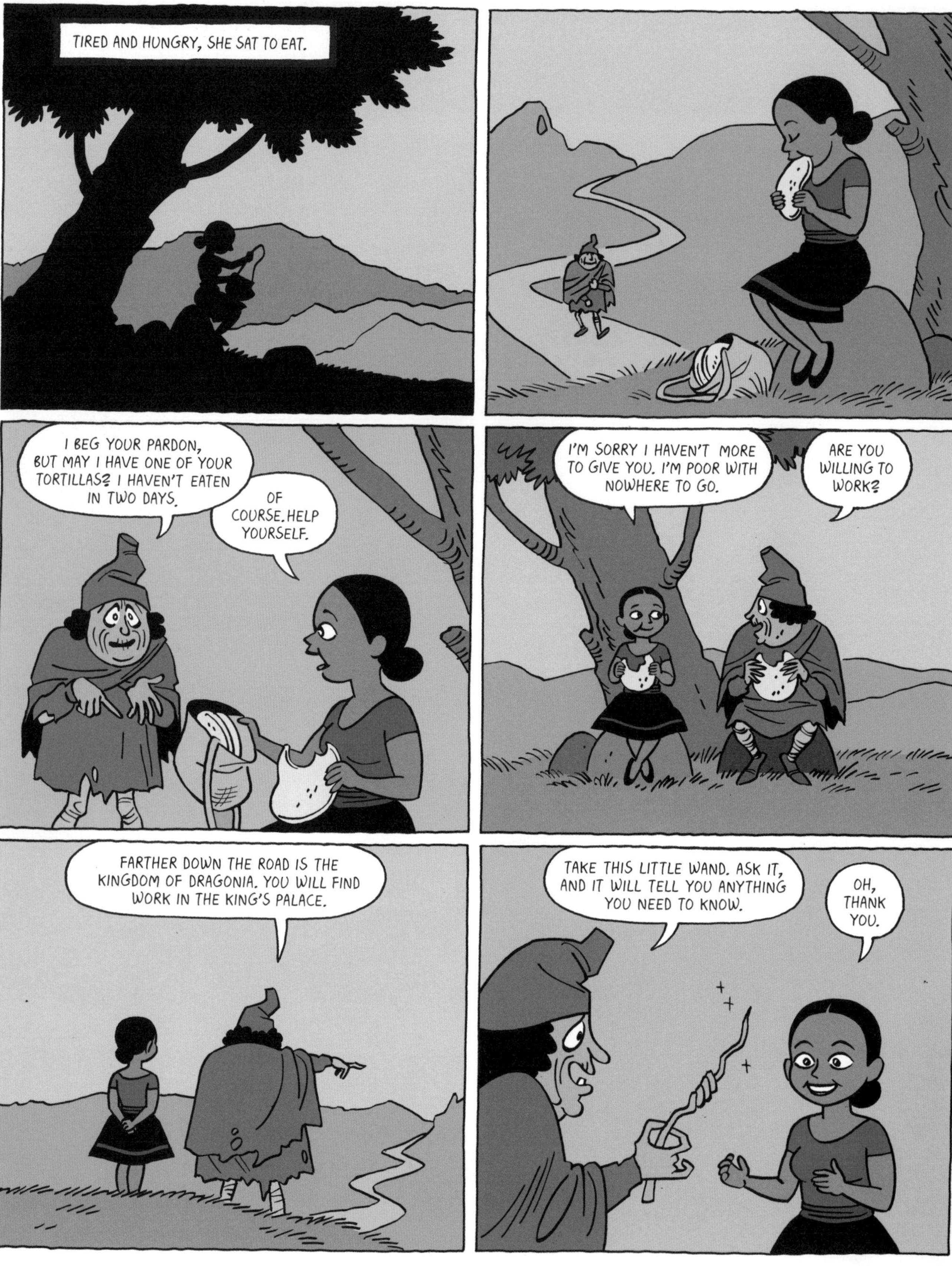
TIRED AND HUNGRY, SHE SAT TO EAT.
I BEG YOUR PARDON, BUT MAY I HAVE ONE OF YOUR TORTILLAS? I HAVEN'T EATEN IN TWO DAYS.
OF COURSE. HELP YOURSELF.
I'M SORRY I HAVEN'T MORE TO GIVE YOU. I'M POOR WITH NOWHERE TO GO.
ARE YOU WILLING TO WORK?
FARTHER DOWN THE ROAD IS THE KINGDOM OF DRAGONIA. YOU WILL FIND WORK IN THE KING'S PALACE.
TAKE THIS LITTLE WAND. ASK IT, AND IT WILL TELL YOU ANYTHING YOU NEED TO KNOW.
OH, THANK YOU.

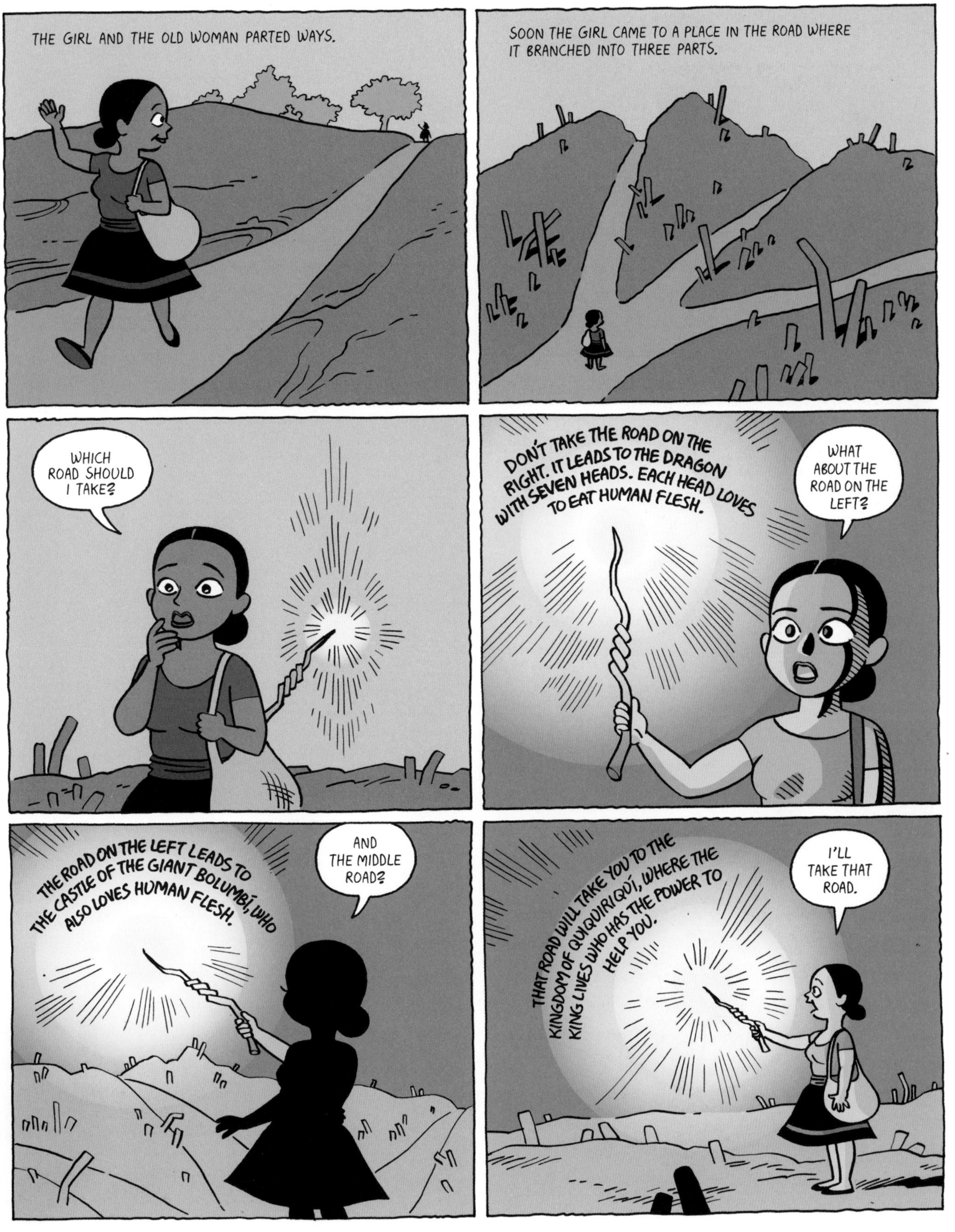
THE GIRL AND THE OLD WOMAN PARTED WAYS.
SOON THE GIRL CAME TO A PLACE IN THE ROAD WHERE IT BRANCHED INTO THREE PARTS.
WHICH ROAD SHOULD I TAKE?
DON'T TAKE THE ROAD ON THE RIGHT. IT LEADS TO THE DRAGON WITH SEVEN HEADS. EACH HEAD LOVES TO EAT HUMAN FLESH.
WHAT ABOUT THE ROAD ON THE LEFT?
THE ROAD ON THE LEFT LEADS TO THE CASTLE OF THE GIANT BOLUMBÍ, WHO ALSO LOVES HUMAN FLESH.
AND THE MIDDLE ROAD?
THAT ROAD WILL TAKE YOU TO THE KINGDOM OF QUIQUIRIQUÍ, WHERE THE KING LIVES WHO HAS THE POWER TO HELP YOU.
I'LL TAKE THAT ROAD.

FILLED WITH HOPE, THE GIRL CONTINUED ON.

AT LAST SHE MADE IT TO THE KING'S PALACE.

IS THERE ANY WORK HERE?

I DON'T KNOW. FOLLOW ME.

YOUR MAJESTY, THIS GIRL IS LOOKING FOR WORK.

SHE CAN WORK IN THE KITCHEN.

SOON, THE GIRL BECAME INTERESTED IN THE KING'S SON, THE PRINCE, BUT KEPT IT TO HERSELF. HE ALSO BECAME INTERESTED IN HER BUT SAID NOTHING.

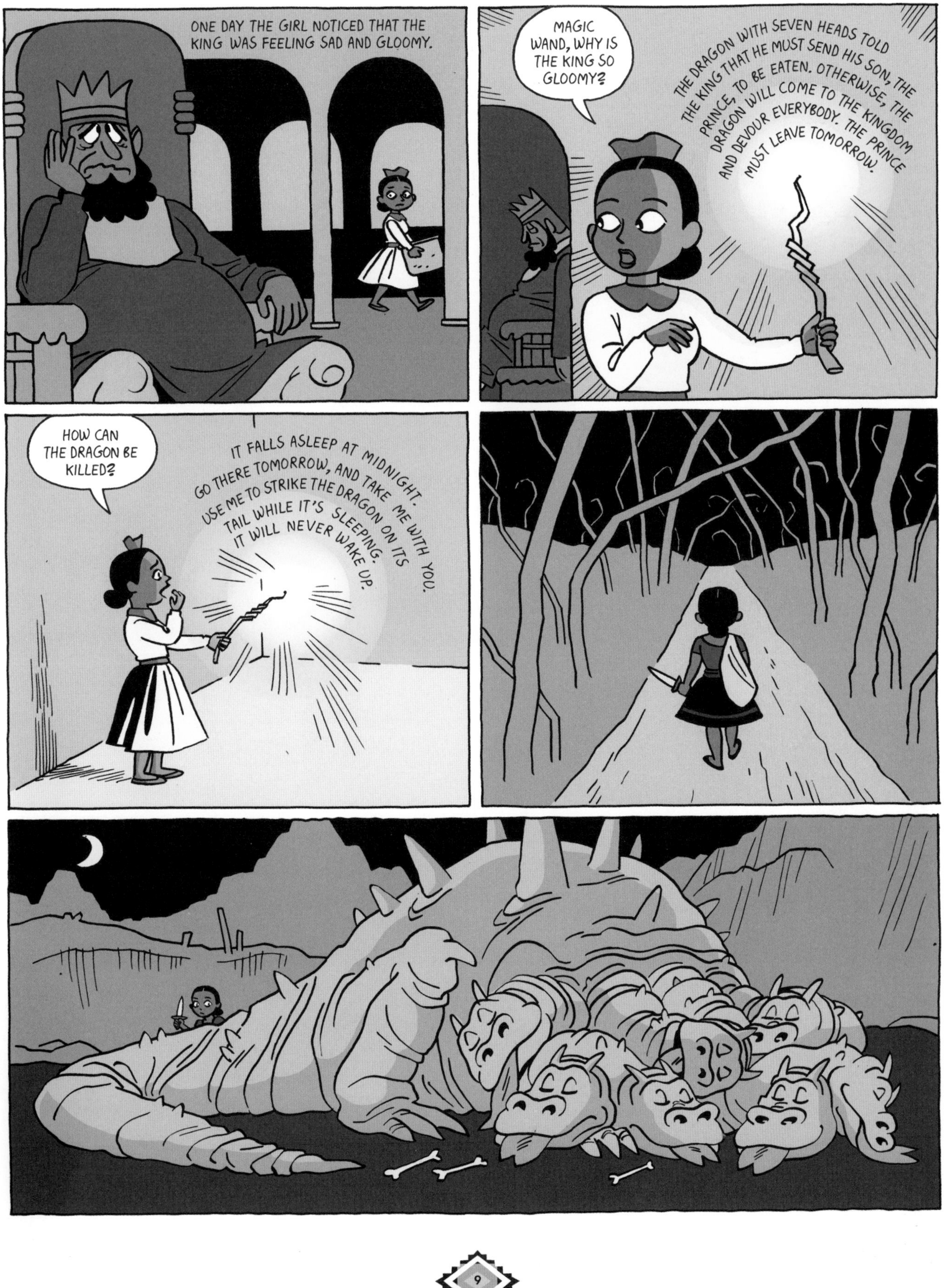

ONE DAY THE GIRL NOTICED THAT THE KING WAS FEELING SAD AND GLOOMY.
MAGIC WAND, WHY IS THE KING SO GLOOMY?
THE DRAGON WITH SEVEN HEADS TOLD THE KING THAT HE MUST SEND HIS SON, THE PRINCE, TO BE EATEN. OTHERWISE, THE DRAGON WILL COME TO THE KINGDOM AND DEVOUR EVERYBODY. THE PRINCE MUST LEAVE TOMORROW.
HOW CAN THE DRAGON BE KILLED?
IT FALLS ASLEEP AT MIDNIGHT. GO THERE TOMORROW, AND TAKE ME WITH YOU. USE ME TO STRIKE THE DRAGON ON ITS TAIL WHILE IT'S SLEEPING. IT WILL NEVER WAKE UP.

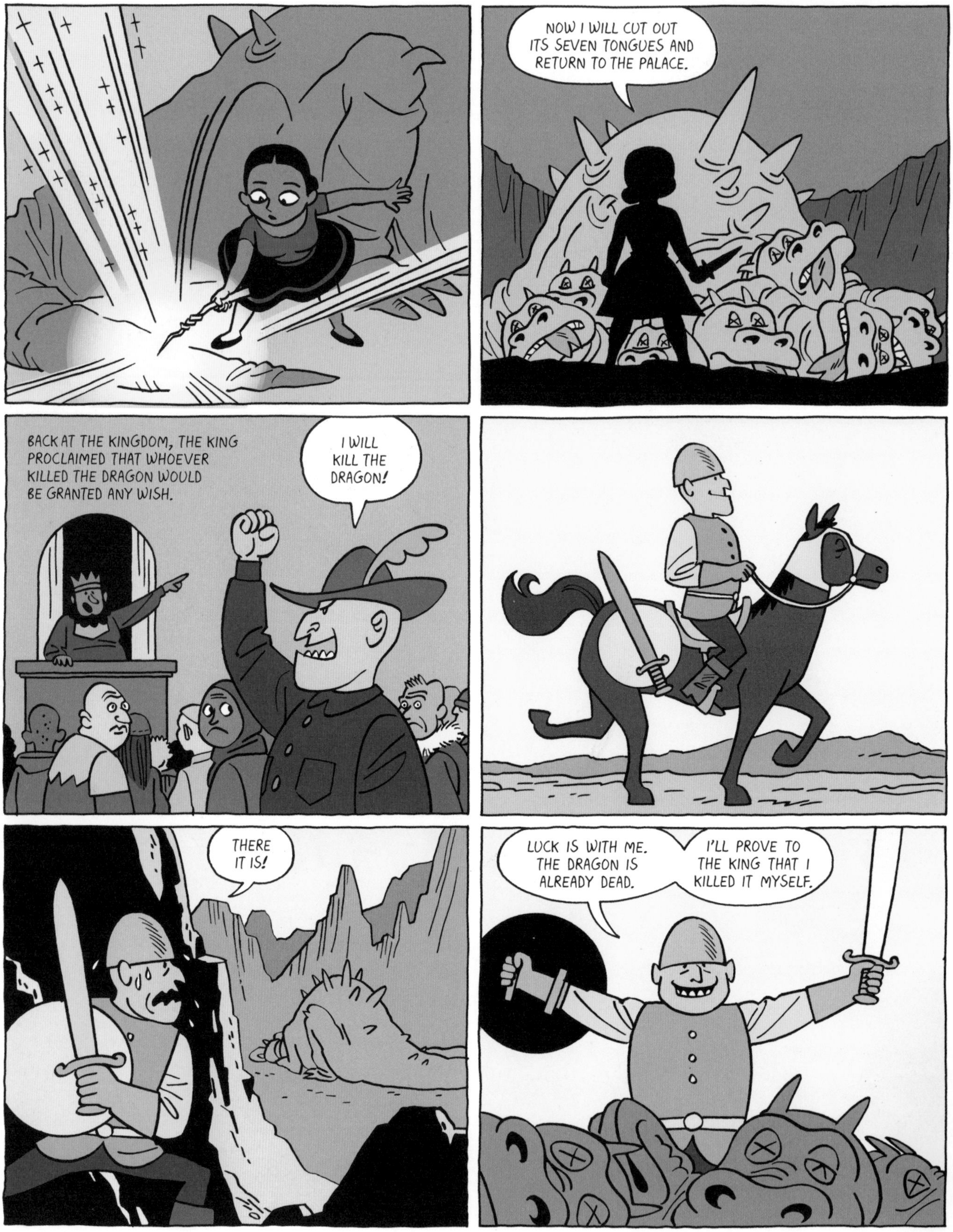
NOW I WILL CUT OUT ITS SEVEN TONGUES AND RETURN TO THE PALACE.
BACK AT THE KINGDOM, THE KING PROCLAIMED THAT WHOEVER KILLED THE DRAGON WOULD BE GRANTED ANY WISH.
I WILL KILL THE DRAGON!
THERE IT IS!
LUCK IS WITH ME. THE DRAGON IS ALREADY DEAD.
I'LL PROVE TO THE KING THAT I KILLED IT MYSELF.

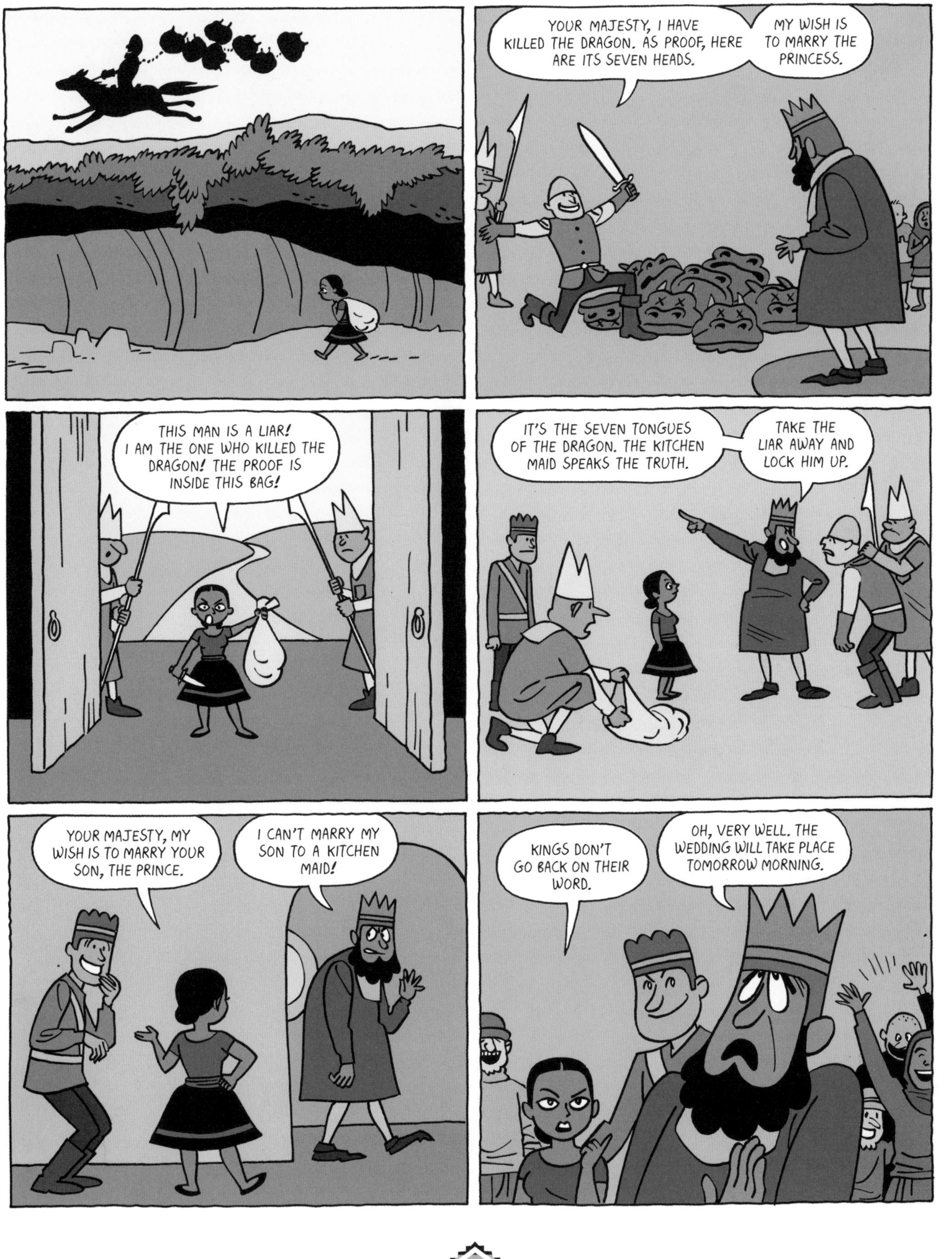
YOUR MAJESTY, I HAVE KILLED THE DRAGON. AS PROOF, HERE ARE ITS SEVEN HEADS.
MY WISH IS TO MARRY THE PRINCESS.
THIS MAN IS A LIAR! I AM THE ONE WHO KILLED THE DRAGON! THE PROOF IS INSIDE THIS BAG!
IT'S THE SEVEN TONGUES OF THE DRAGON. THE KITCHEN MAID SPEAKS THE TRUTH.
TAKE THE LIAR AWAY AND LOCK HIM UP.
YOUR MAJESTY, MY WISH IS TO MARRY YOUR SON, THE PRINCE.
I CAN'T MARRY MY SON TO A KITCHEN MAID!
KINGS DON'T GO BACK ON THEIR WORD.
OH, VERY WELL. THE WEDDING WILL TAKE PLACE TOMORROW MORNING.

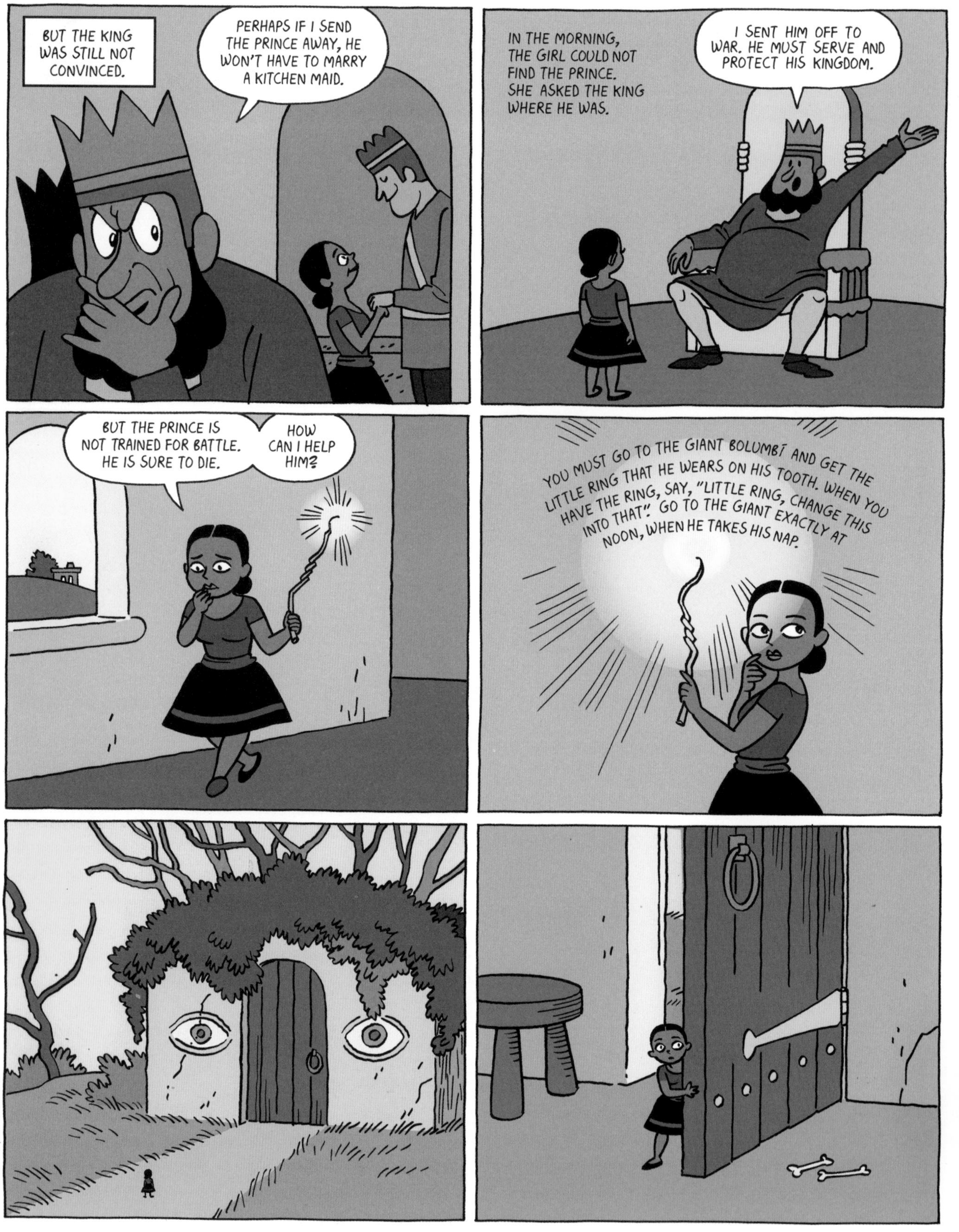

BUT THE KING WAS STILL NOT CONVINCED.
PERHAPS IF I SEND THE PRINCE AWAY, HE WON'T HAVE TO MARRY A KITCHEN MAID.
IN THE MORNING, THE GIRL COULD NOT FIND THE PRINCE. SHE ASKED THE KING WHERE HE WAS.
I SENT HIM OFF TO WAR. HE MUST SERVE AND PROTECT HIS KINGDOM.
BUT THE PRINCE IS NOT TRAINED FOR BATTLE. HE IS SURE TO DIE.
HOW CAN I HELP HIM?
YOU MUST GO TO THE GIANT BOLUMBĪ AND GET THE LITTLE RING THAT HE WEARS ON HIS TOOTH. WHEN YOU HAVE THE RING, SAY, "LITTLE RING, CHANGE THIS INTO THAT." GO TO THE GIANT EXACTLY AT NOON, WHEN HE TAKES HIS NAP.

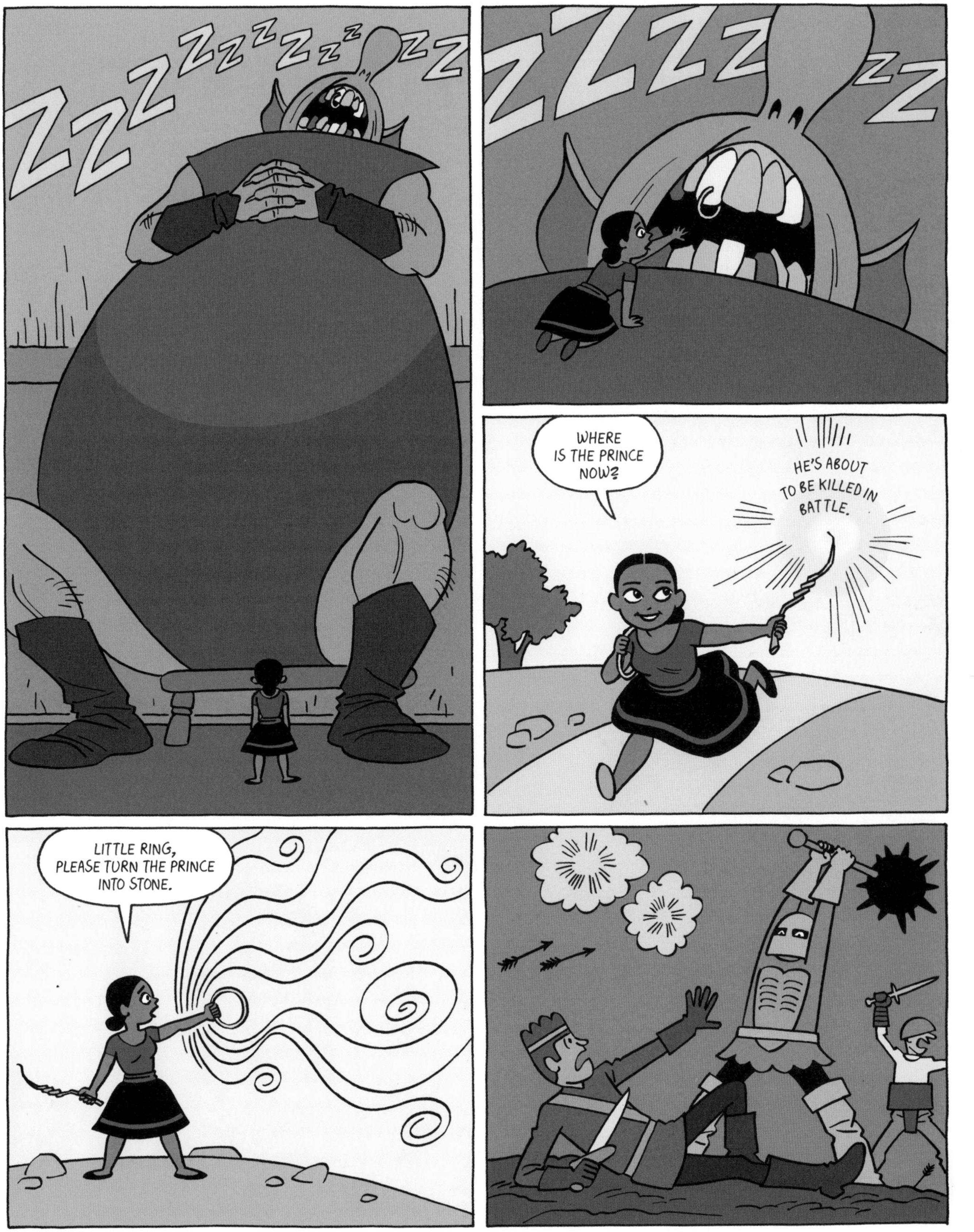
ZZZZZZZZZZZZ
ZZZZZZ
WHERE IS THE PRINCE NOW?
HE'S ABOUT TO BE KILLED IN BATTLE.
LITTLE RING, PLEASE TURN THE PRINCE INTO STONE.

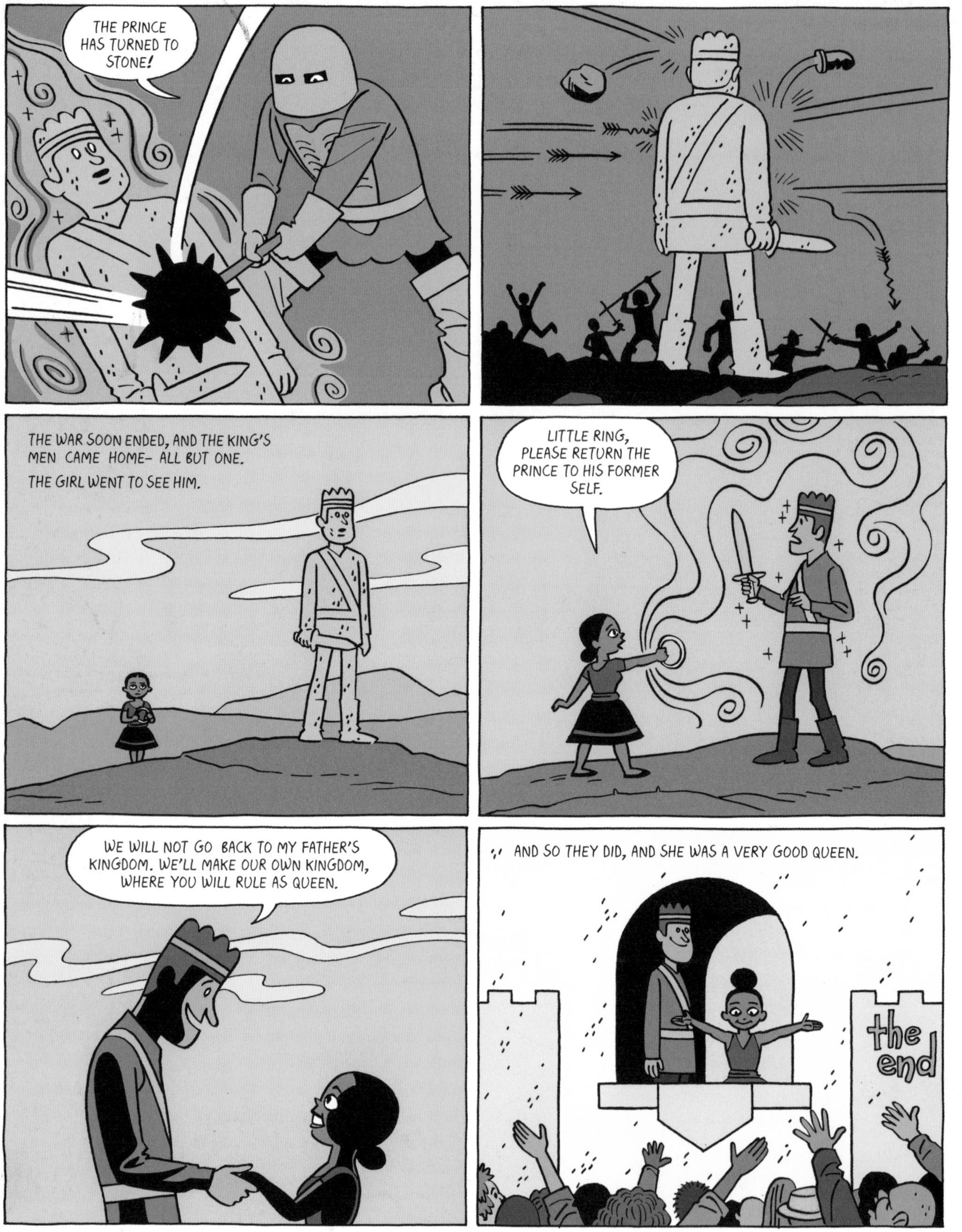
THE PRINCE HAS TURNED TO STONE!
THE WAR SOON ENDED, AND THE KING'S MEN CAME HOME– ALL BUT ONE.
THE GIRL WENT TO SEE HIM.
LITTLE RING, PLEASE RETURN THE PRINCE TO HIS FORMER SELF.
WE WILL NOT GO BACK TO MY FATHER'S KINGDOM. WE'LL MAKE OUR OWN KINGDOM, WHERE YOU WILL RULE AS QUEEN.
AND SO THEY DID, AND SHE WAS A VERY GOOD QUEEN.
the end

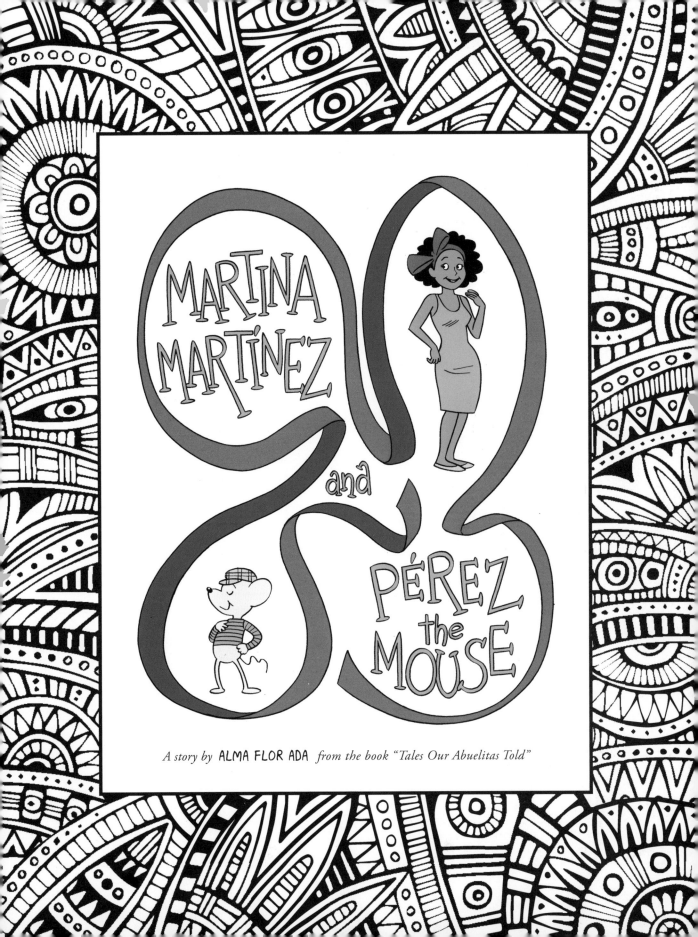

MARTINA MARTÍNEZ and PÉREZ the MOUSE

A story by **ALMA FLOR ADA** *from the book "Tales Our Abuelitas Told"*

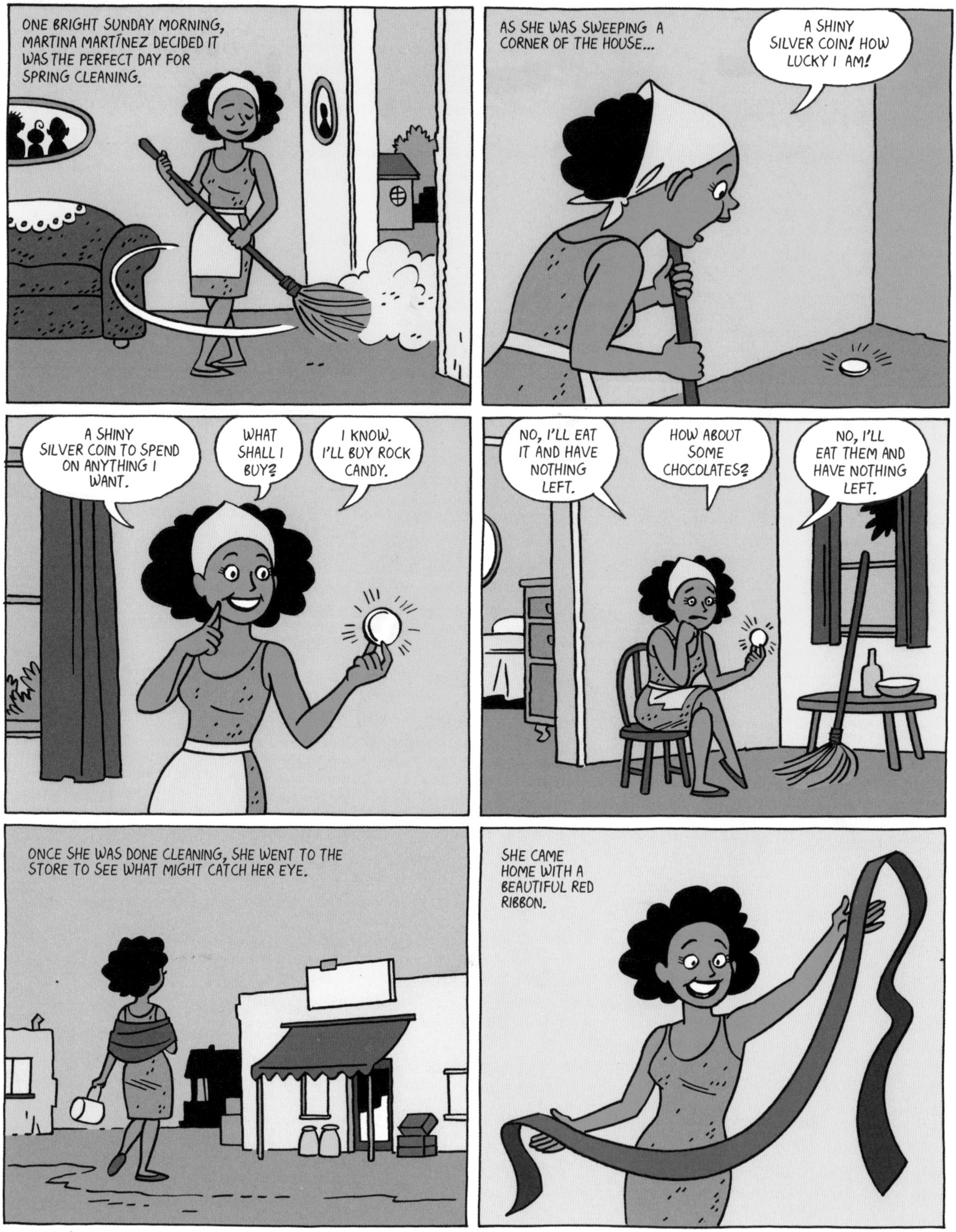
ONE BRIGHT SUNDAY MORNING, MARTINA MARTÍNEZ DECIDED IT WAS THE PERFECT DAY FOR SPRING CLEANING.
AS SHE WAS SWEEPING A CORNER OF THE HOUSE...
A SHINY SILVER COIN! HOW LUCKY I AM!
A SHINY SILVER COIN TO SPEND ON ANYTHING I WANT.
WHAT SHALL I BUY?
I KNOW. I'LL BUY ROCK CANDY.
NO, I'LL EAT IT AND HAVE NOTHING LEFT.
HOW ABOUT SOME CHOCOLATES?
NO, I'LL EAT THEM AND HAVE NOTHING LEFT.
ONCE SHE WAS DONE CLEANING, SHE WENT TO THE STORE TO SEE WHAT MIGHT CATCH HER EYE.
SHE CAME HOME WITH A BEAUTIFUL RED RIBBON.

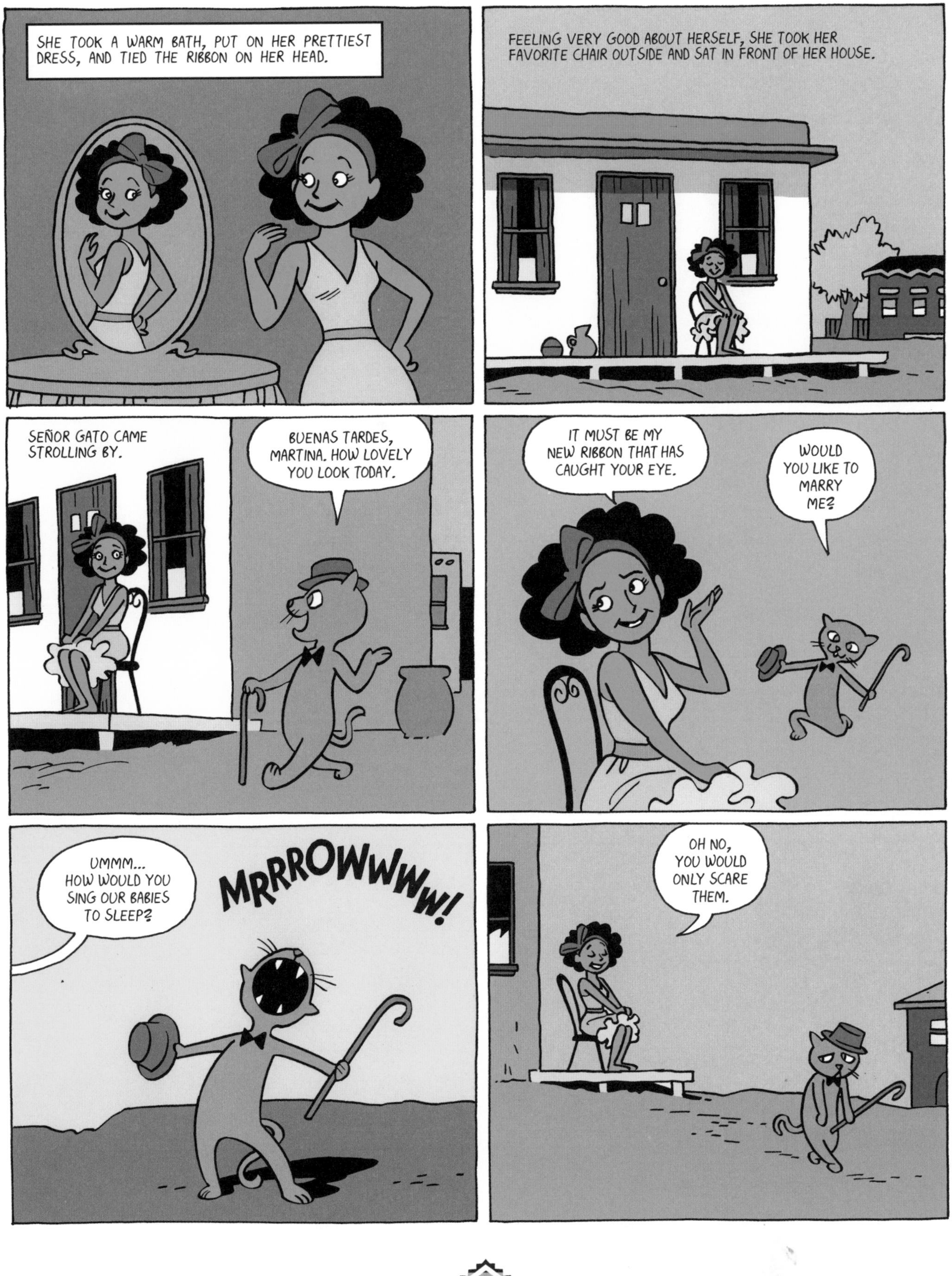
SHE TOOK A WARM BATH, PUT ON HER PRETTIEST DRESS, AND TIED THE RIBBON ON HER HEAD.
FEELING VERY GOOD ABOUT HERSELF, SHE TOOK HER FAVORITE CHAIR OUTSIDE AND SAT IN FRONT OF HER HOUSE.
SEÑOR GATO CAME STROLLING BY.
BUENAS TARDES, MARTINA. HOW LOVELY YOU LOOK TODAY.
IT MUST BE MY NEW RIBBON THAT HAS CAUGHT YOUR EYE.
WOULD YOU LIKE TO MARRY ME?
UMMM... HOW WOULD YOU SING OUR BABIES TO SLEEP?
MRRROWWWW!
OH NO, YOU WOULD ONLY SCARE THEM.

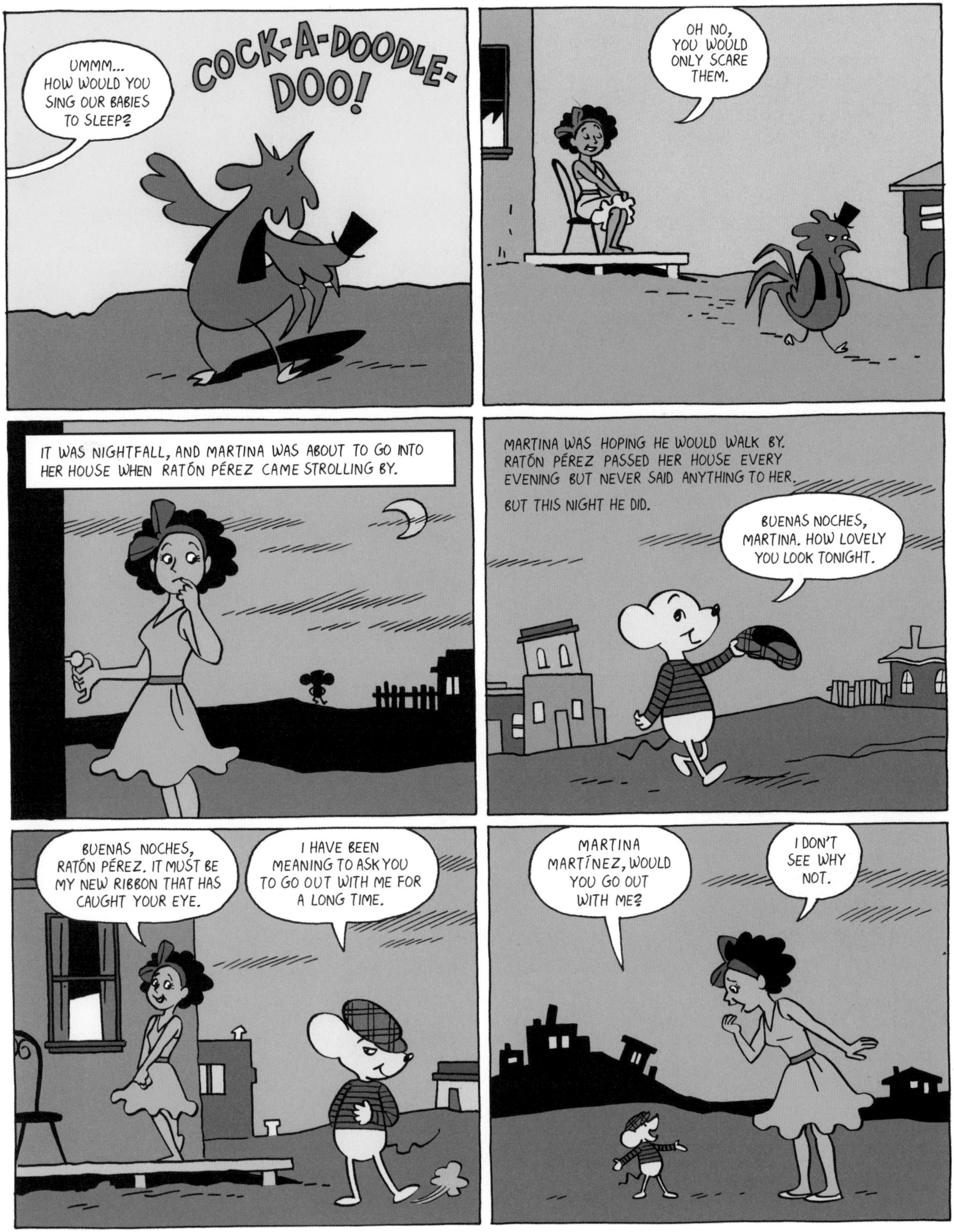
UMMM... HOW WOULD YOU SING OUR BABIES TO SLEEP?
COCK-A-DOODLE-DOO!
OH NO, YOU WOULD ONLY SCARE THEM.
IT WAS NIGHTFALL, AND MARTINA WAS ABOUT TO GO INTO HER HOUSE WHEN RATÓN PÉREZ CAME STROLLING BY.
MARTINA WAS HOPING HE WOULD WALK BY. RATÓN PÉREZ PASSED HER HOUSE EVERY EVENING BUT NEVER SAID ANYTHING TO HER.
BUT THIS NIGHT HE DID.
BUENAS NOCHES, MARTINA. HOW LOVELY YOU LOOK TONIGHT.
BUENAS NOCHES, RATÓN PÉREZ. IT MUST BE MY NEW RIBBON THAT HAS CAUGHT YOUR EYE.
I HAVE BEEN MEANING TO ASK YOU TO GO OUT WITH ME FOR A LONG TIME.
MARTINA MARTÍNEZ, WOULD YOU GO OUT WITH ME?
I DON'T SEE WHY NOT.

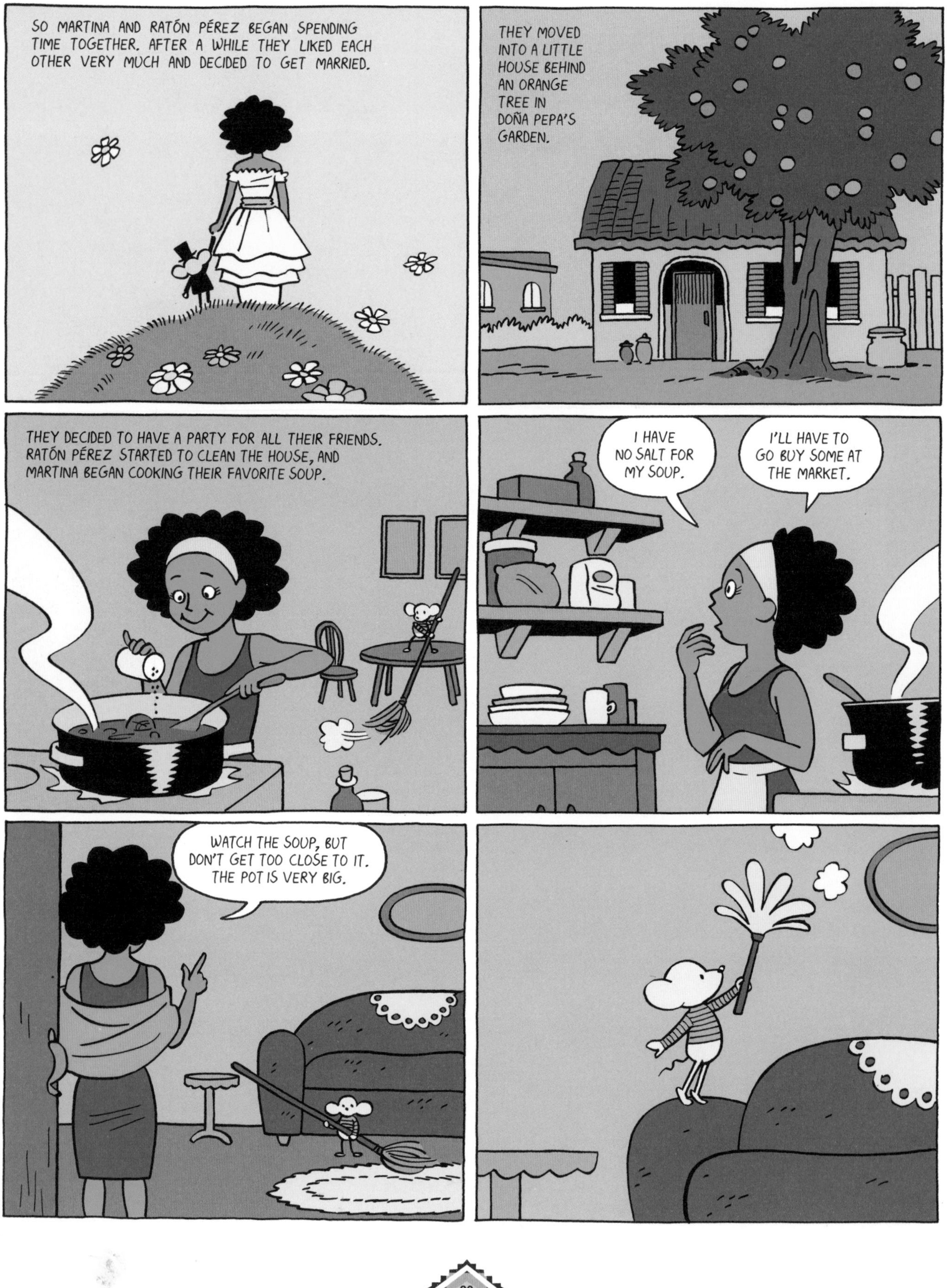
SO MARTINA AND RATÓN PÉREZ BEGAN SPENDING TIME TOGETHER. AFTER A WHILE THEY LIKED EACH OTHER VERY MUCH AND DECIDED TO GET MARRIED.
THEY MOVED INTO A LITTLE HOUSE BEHIND AN ORANGE TREE IN DOÑA PEPA'S GARDEN.
THEY DECIDED TO HAVE A PARTY FOR ALL THEIR FRIENDS. RATÓN PÉREZ STARTED TO CLEAN THE HOUSE, AND MARTINA BEGAN COOKING THEIR FAVORITE SOUP.
I HAVE NO SALT FOR MY SOUP.
I'LL HAVE TO GO BUY SOME AT THE MARKET.
WATCH THE SOUP, BUT DON'T GET TOO CLOSE TO IT. THE POT IS VERY BIG.

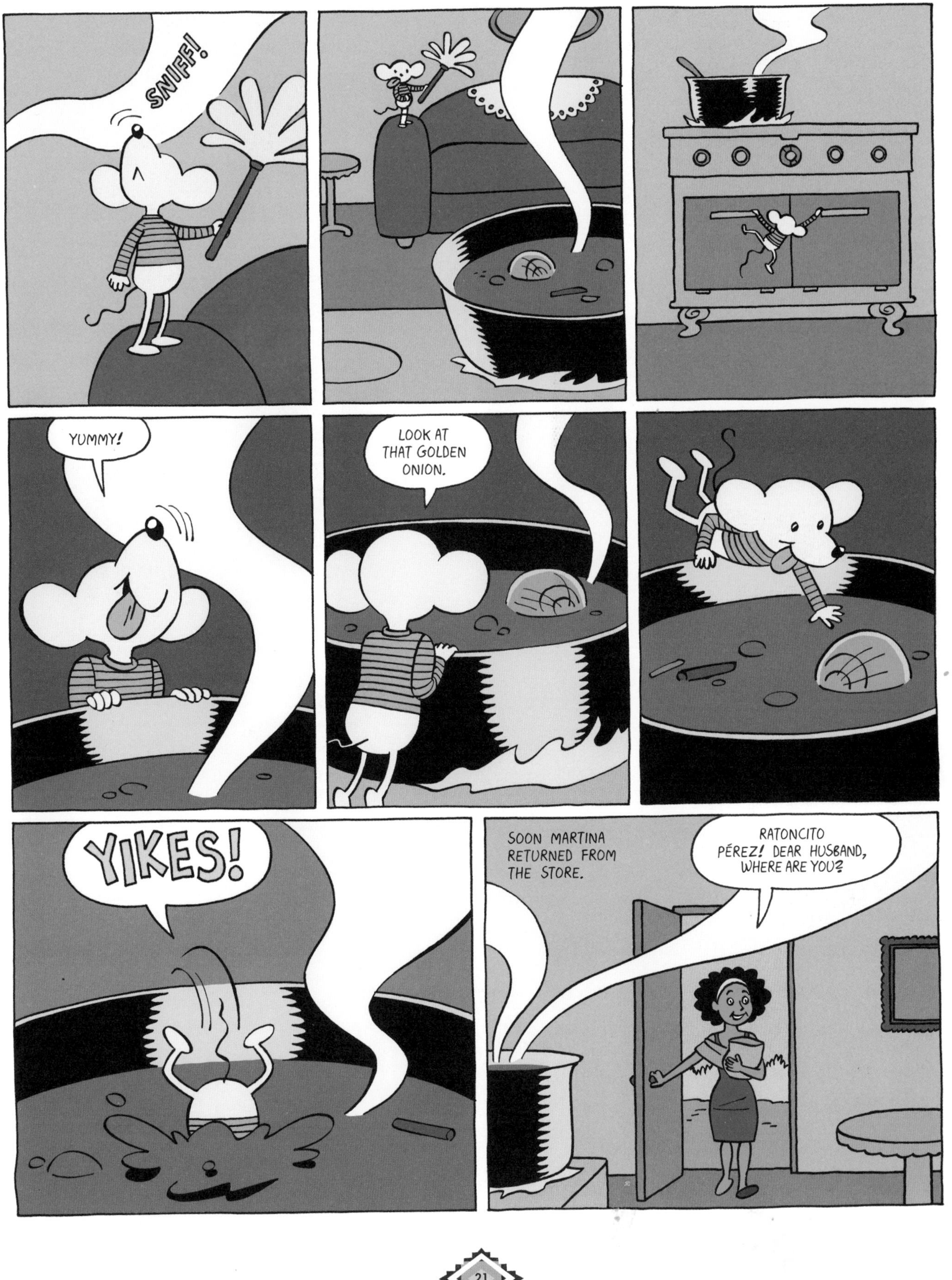
SNIFF!
YUMMY!
LOOK AT THAT GOLDEN ONION.
YIKES!
SOON MARTINA RETURNED FROM THE STORE.
RATONCITO PÉREZ! DEAR HUSBAND, WHERE ARE YOU?

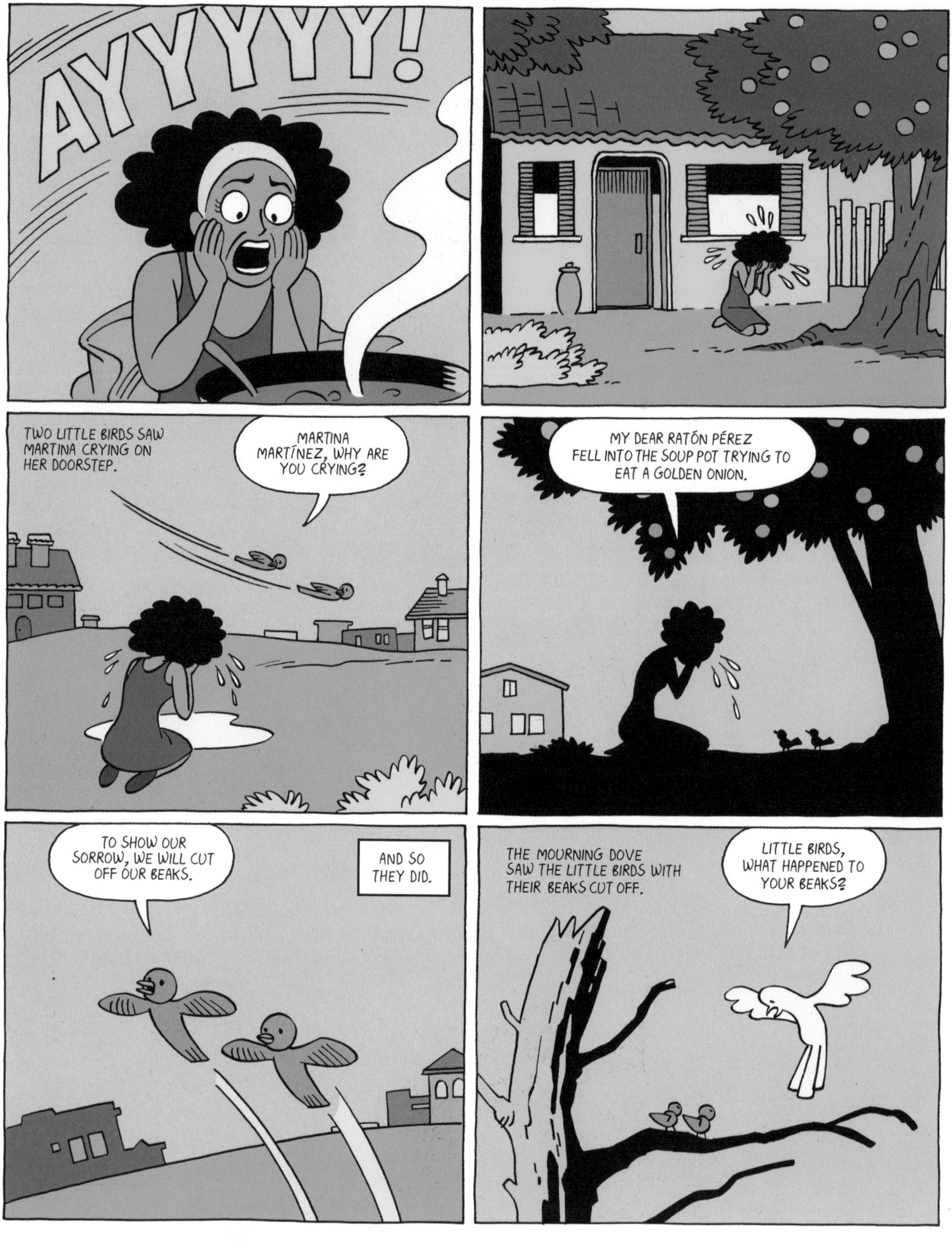
AYYYYY!
TWO LITTLE BIRDS SAW MARTINA CRYING ON HER DOORSTEP.
MARTINA MARTÍNEZ, WHY ARE YOU CRYING?
MY DEAR RATÓN PÉREZ FELL INTO THE SOUP POT TRYING TO EAT A GOLDEN ONION.
TO SHOW OUR SORROW, WE WILL CUT OFF OUR BEAKS.
AND SO THEY DID.
THE MOURNING DOVE SAW THE LITTLE BIRDS WITH THEIR BEAKS CUT OFF.
LITTLE BIRDS, WHAT HAPPENED TO YOUR BEAKS?

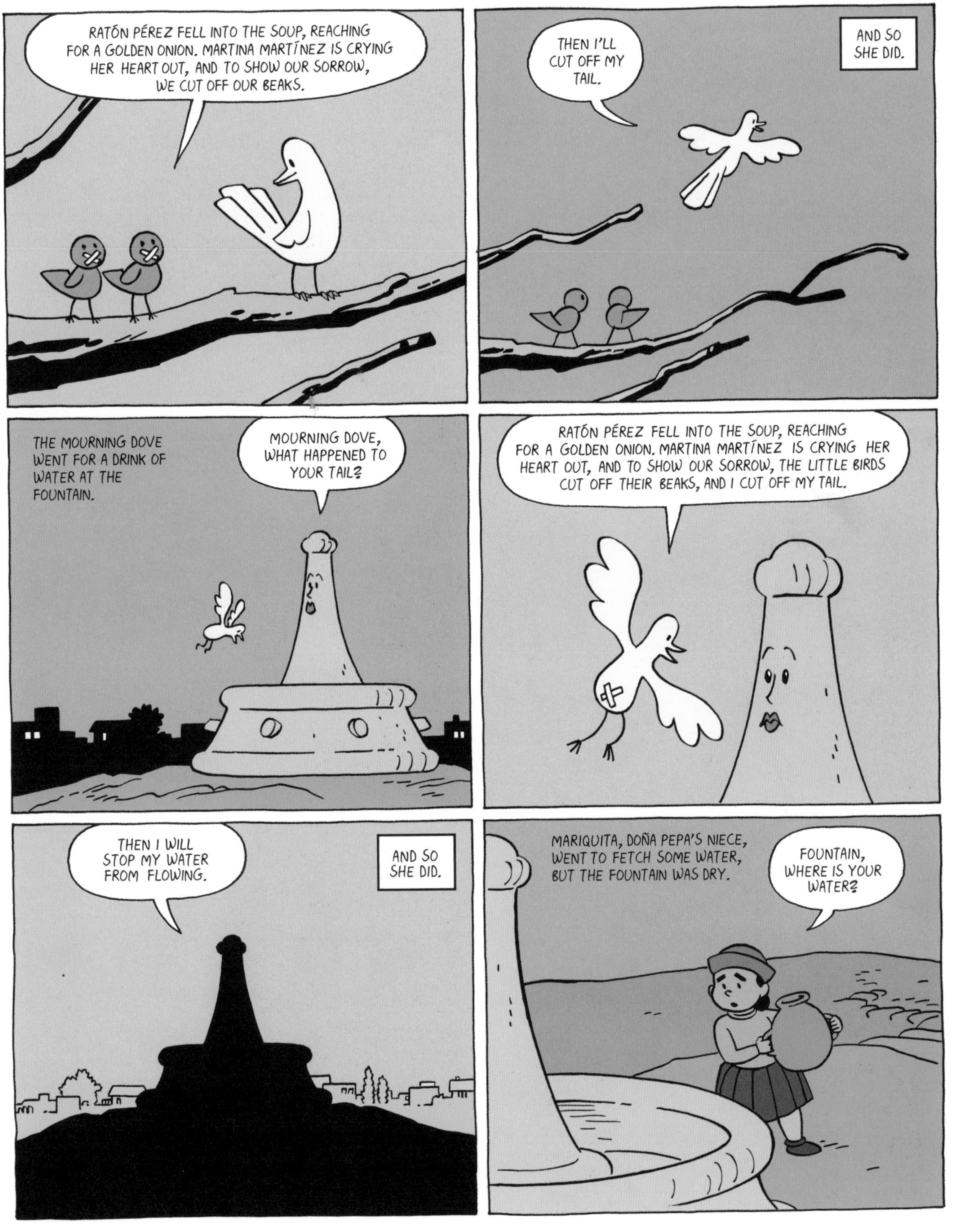
RATÓN PÉREZ FELL INTO THE SOUP, REACHING FOR A GOLDEN ONION. MARTINA MARTÍNEZ IS CRYING HER HEART OUT, AND TO SHOW OUR SORROW, WE CUT OFF OUR BEAKS.
THEN I'LL CUT OFF MY TAIL.
AND SO SHE DID.
THE MOURNING DOVE WENT FOR A DRINK OF WATER AT THE FOUNTAIN.
MOURNING DOVE, WHAT HAPPENED TO YOUR TAIL?
RATÓN PÉREZ FELL INTO THE SOUP, REACHING FOR A GOLDEN ONION. MARTINA MARTÍNEZ IS CRYING HER HEART OUT, AND TO SHOW OUR SORROW, THE LITTLE BIRDS CUT OFF THEIR BEAKS, AND I CUT OFF MY TAIL.
THEN I WILL STOP MY WATER FROM FLOWING.
AND SO SHE DID.
MARIQUITA, DOÑA PEPA'S NIECE, WENT TO FETCH SOME WATER, BUT THE FOUNTAIN WAS DRY.
FOUNTAIN, WHERE IS YOUR WATER?

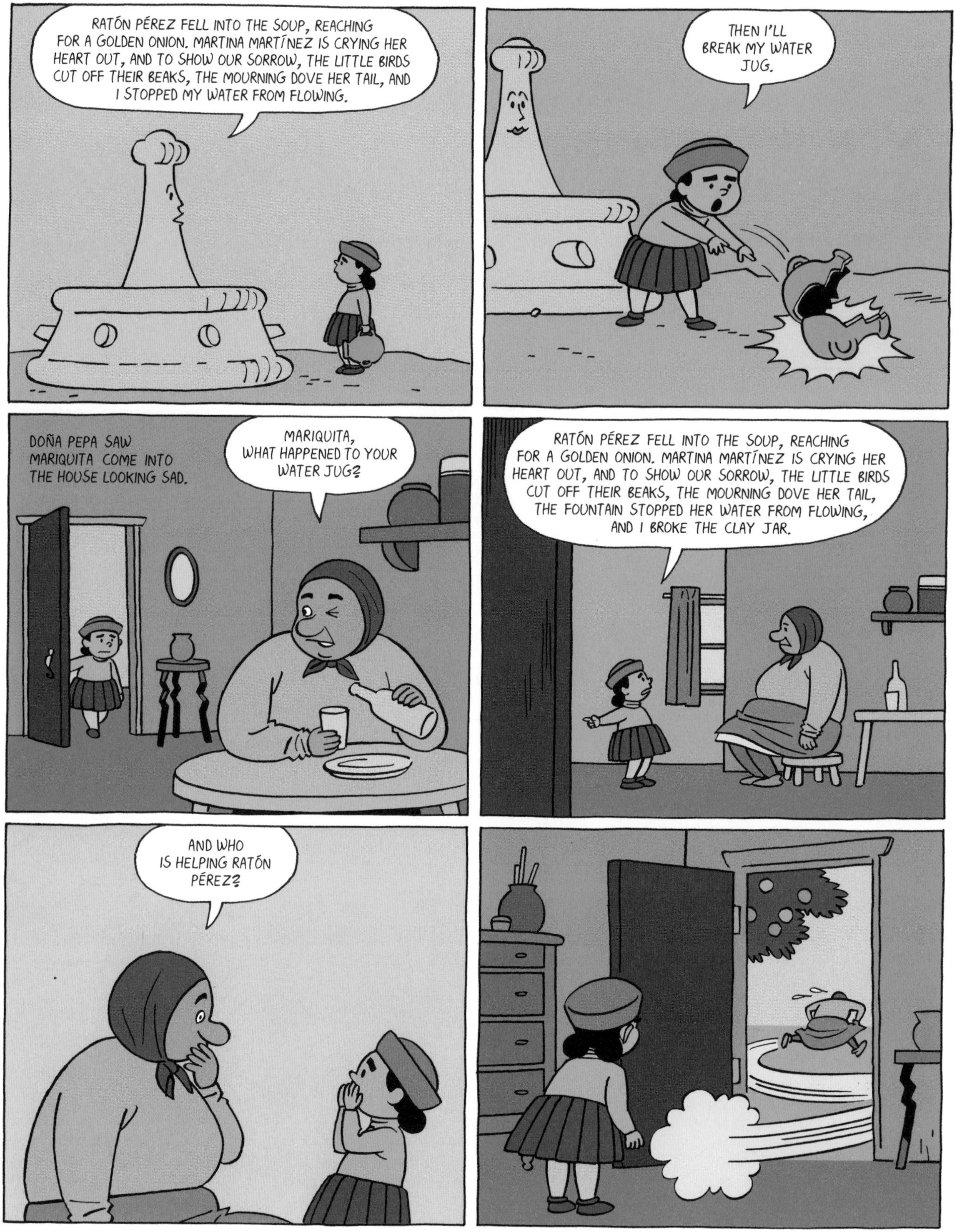
RATÓN PÉREZ FELL INTO THE SOUP, REACHING FOR A GOLDEN ONION. MARTINA MARTÍNEZ IS CRYING HER HEART OUT, AND TO SHOW OUR SORROW, THE LITTLE BIRDS CUT OFF THEIR BEAKS, THE MOURNING DOVE HER TAIL, AND I STOPPED MY WATER FROM FLOWING.
THEN I'LL BREAK MY WATER JUG.
DOÑA PEPA SAW MARIQUITA COME INTO THE HOUSE LOOKING SAD.
MARIQUITA, WHAT HAPPENED TO YOUR WATER JUG?
RATÓN PÉREZ FELL INTO THE SOUP, REACHING FOR A GOLDEN ONION. MARTINA MARTÍNEZ IS CRYING HER HEART OUT, AND TO SHOW OUR SORROW, THE LITTLE BIRDS CUT OFF THEIR BEAKS, THE MOURNING DOVE HER TAIL, THE FOUNTAIN STOPPED HER WATER FROM FLOWING, AND I BROKE THE CLAY JAR.
AND WHO IS HELPING RATÓN PÉREZ?

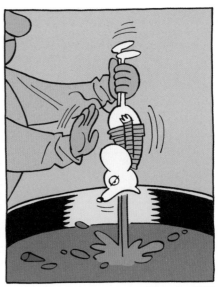

RATÓN PÉREZ WAS SAVED AND PUT TO BED TO REST.

DOÑA PEPA HELPED MARTINA MAKE SOME FLOUR PASTE FOR THE LITTLE BIRDS' BEAKS, THE MOURNING DOVE'S TAIL, AND MARIQUITA'S WATER JAR.

THEY ALL WENT TO ASK THE FOUNTAIN TO MAKE HER WATER RUN AGAIN AND ANNOUNCED THAT THERE WOULD BE A PARTY THAT NIGHT.

AND THEY HAD A GREAT BIG FIESTA.

THE END

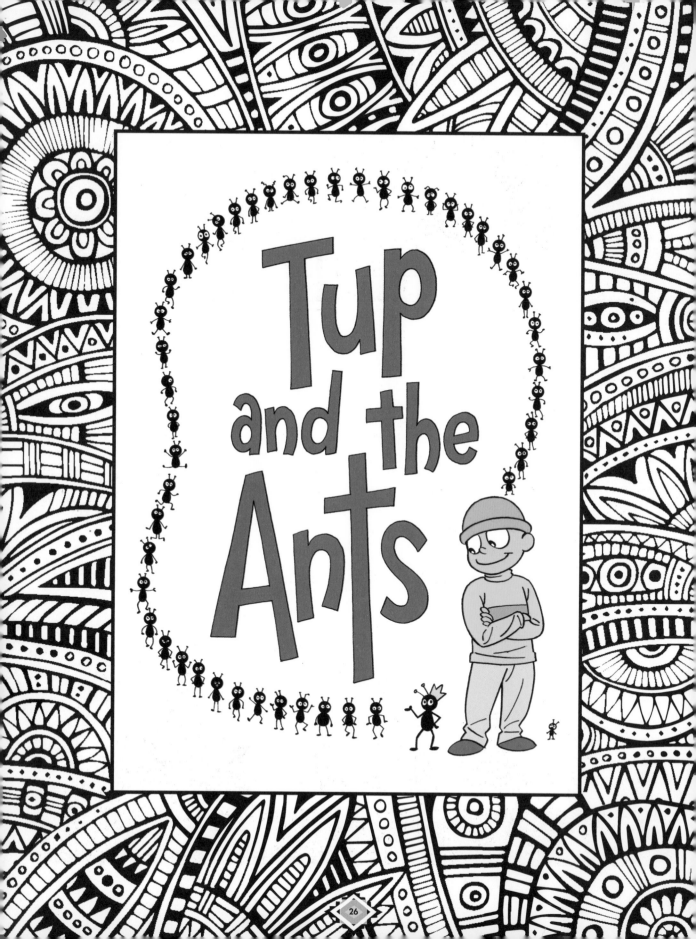

Tup and the Ants

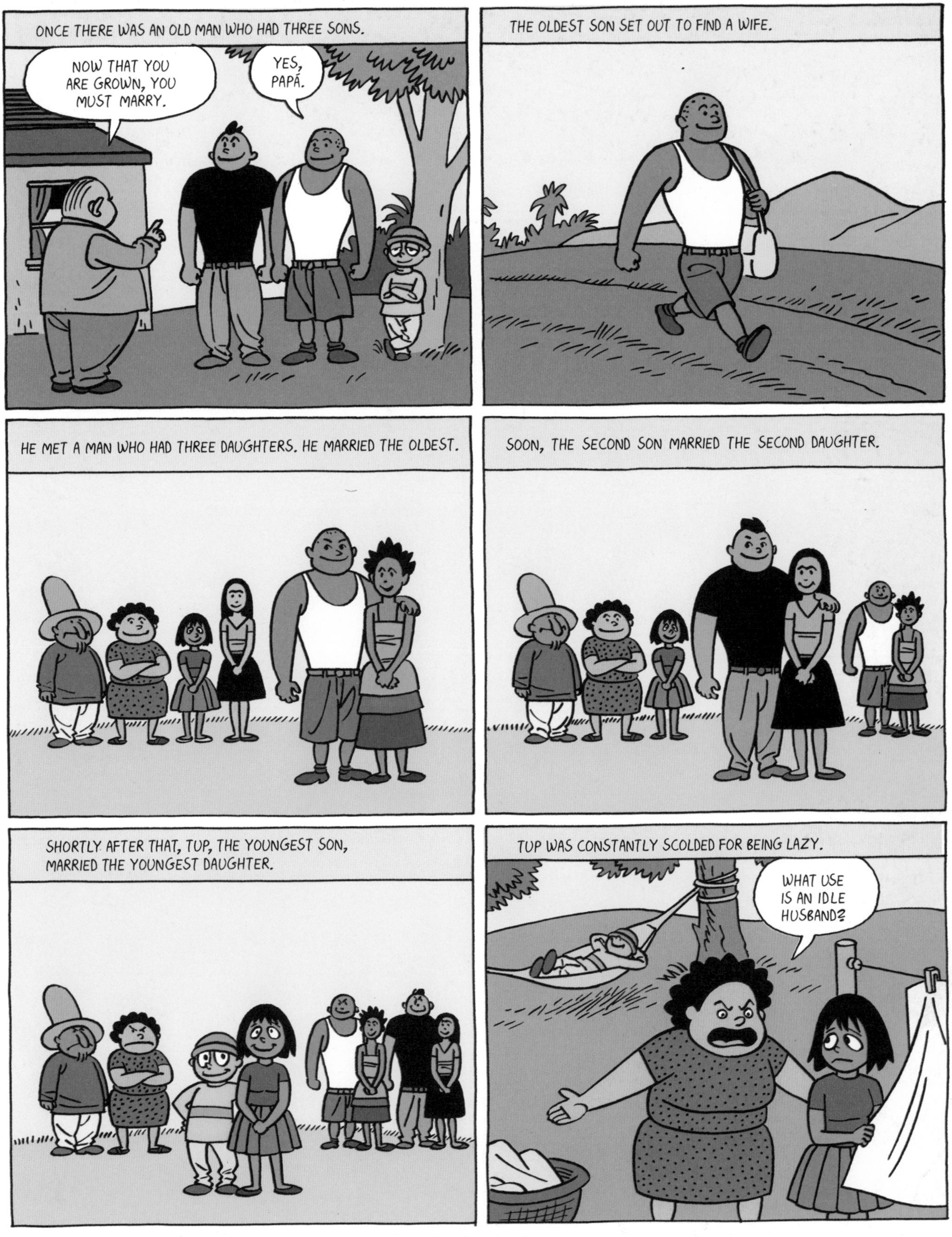
ONCE THERE WAS AN OLD MAN WHO HAD THREE SONS.
NOW THAT YOU ARE GROWN, YOU MUST MARRY.
YES, PAPÁ.
THE OLDEST SON SET OUT TO FIND A WIFE.
HE MET A MAN WHO HAD THREE DAUGHTERS. HE MARRIED THE OLDEST.
SOON, THE SECOND SON MARRIED THE SECOND DAUGHTER.
SHORTLY AFTER THAT, TUP, THE YOUNGEST SON, MARRIED THE YOUNGEST DAUGHTER.
TUP WAS CONSTANTLY SCOLDED FOR BEING LAZY.
WHAT USE IS AN IDLE HUSBAND?

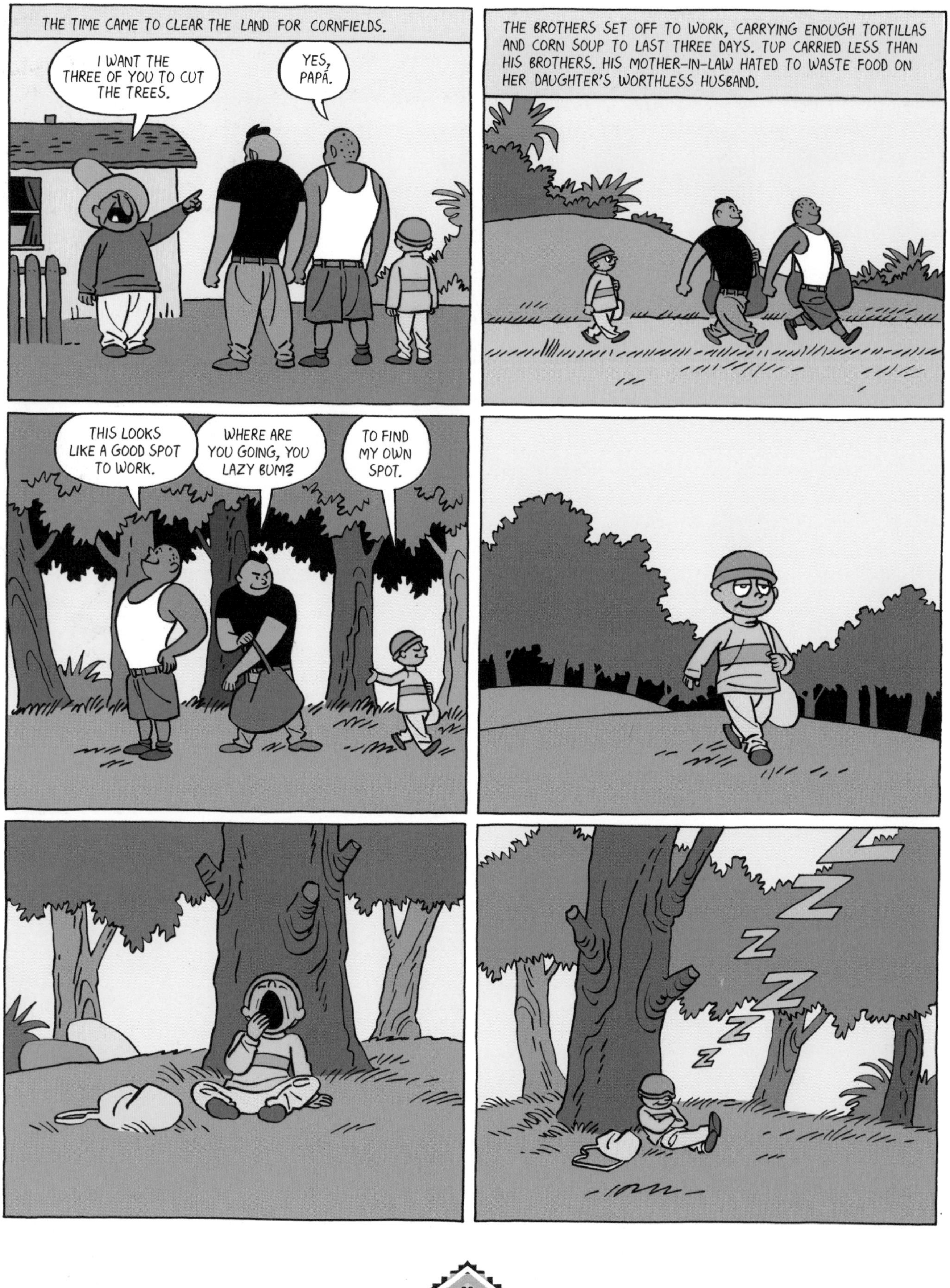
THE TIME CAME TO CLEAR THE LAND FOR CORNFIELDS.
I WANT THE THREE OF YOU TO CUT THE TREES.
YES, PAPÁ.
THE BROTHERS SET OFF TO WORK, CARRYING ENOUGH TORTILLAS AND CORN SOUP TO LAST THREE DAYS. TUP CARRIED LESS THAN HIS BROTHERS. HIS MOTHER-IN-LAW HATED TO WASTE FOOD ON HER DAUGHTER'S WORTHLESS HUSBAND.
THIS LOOKS LIKE A GOOD SPOT TO WORK.
WHERE ARE YOU GOING, YOU LAZY BUM?
TO FIND MY OWN SPOT.
Z Z Z Z Z Z

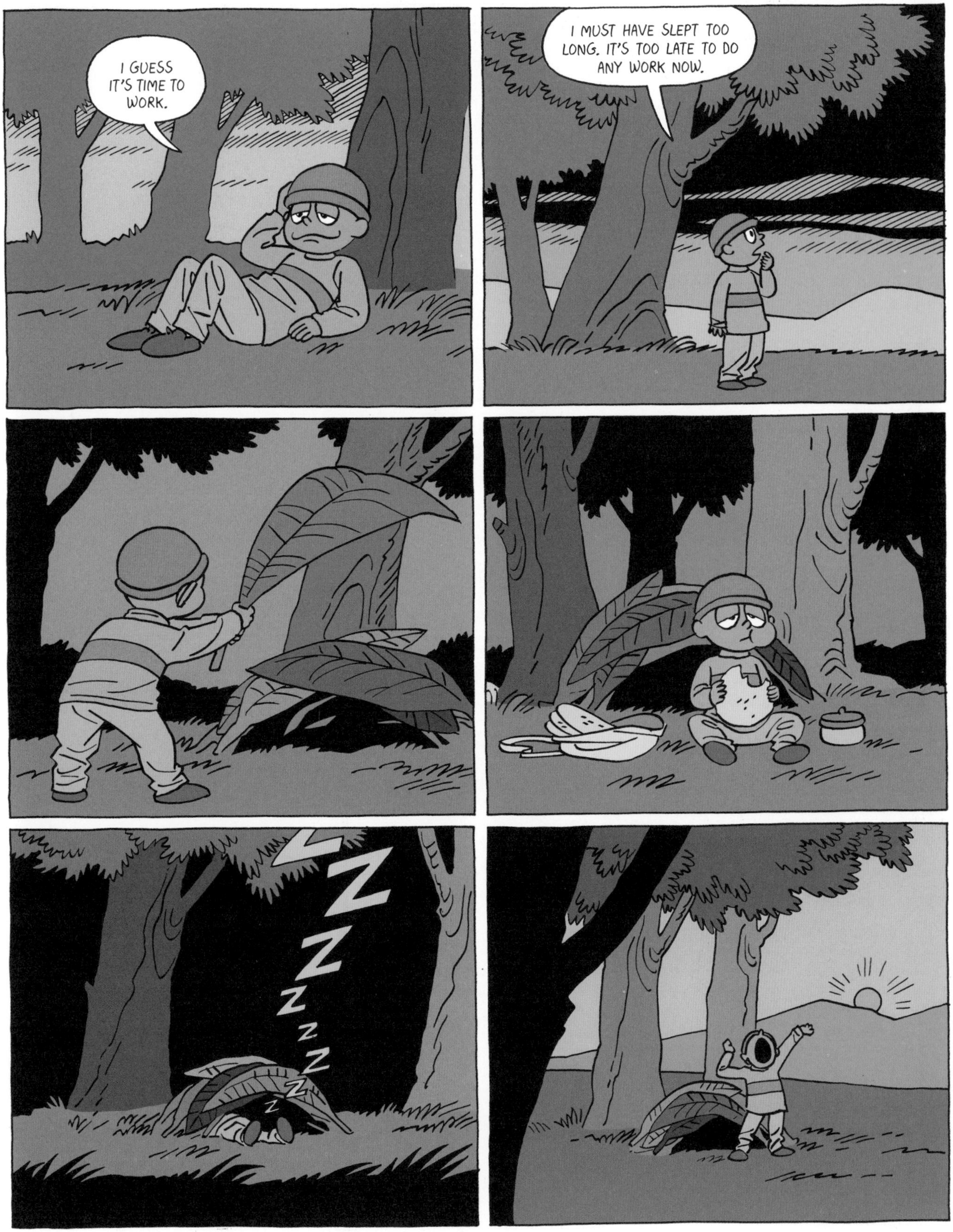
I GUESS IT'S TIME TO WORK.
I MUST HAVE SLEPT TOO LONG. IT'S TOO LATE TO DO ANY WORK NOW.
ZZZZZZZ

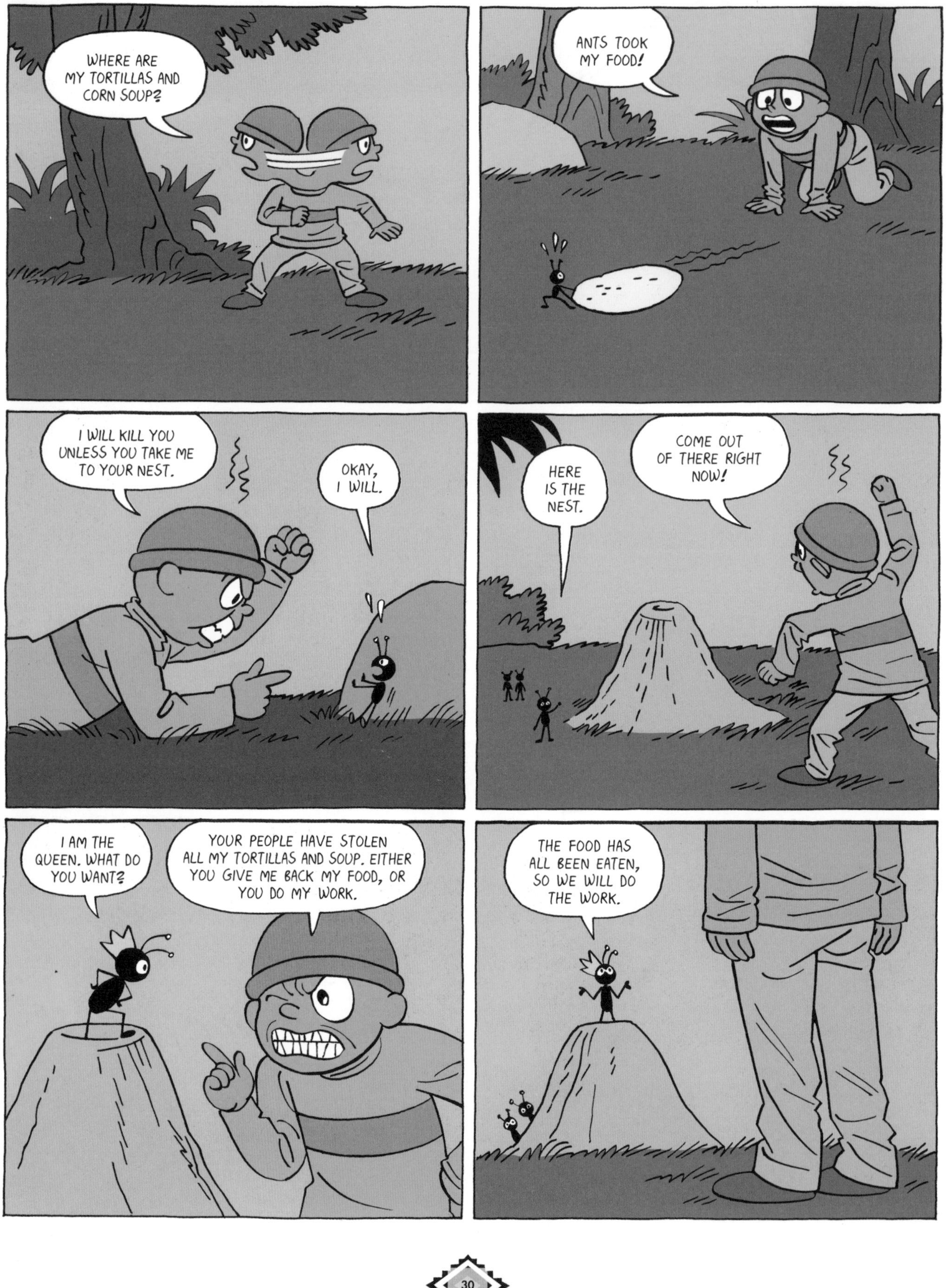
WHERE ARE MY TORTILLAS AND CORN SOUP?
ANTS TOOK MY FOOD!
I WILL KILL YOU UNLESS YOU TAKE ME TO YOUR NEST.
OKAY, I WILL.
HERE IS THE NEST.
COME OUT OF THERE RIGHT NOW!
I AM THE QUEEN. WHAT DO YOU WANT?
YOUR PEOPLE HAVE STOLEN ALL MY TORTILLAS AND SOUP. EITHER YOU GIVE ME BACK MY FOOD, OR YOU DO MY WORK.
THE FOOD HAS ALL BEEN EATEN, SO WE WILL DO THE WORK.

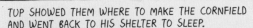

TUP SHOWED THEM WHERE TO MAKE THE CORNFIELD AND WENT BACK TO HIS SHELTER TO SLEEP.

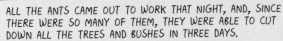

ALL THE ANTS CAME OUT TO WORK THAT NIGHT, AND, SINCE THERE WERE SO MANY OF THEM, THEY WERE ABLE TO CUT DOWN ALL THE TREES AND BUSHES IN THREE DAYS.

WITH ALL THAT DONE, I CAN HEAD BACK HOME.

I WONDER HOW MY BROTHERS ARE DOING.

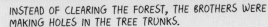

INSTEAD OF CLEARING THE FOREST, THE BROTHERS WERE MAKING HOLES IN THE TREE TRUNKS.

WHAT FOOLS! WHEN THE OLD MAN SAID, "CUT TREES," HE MEANT CUT THEM DOWN, NOT JUST "CUT THEM."

HERE COMES LAZY BONES, THE LAST TO GO AND THE FIRST TO RETURN.

DON'T GIVE HIM ANYTHING TO EAT.

AND HERE COME MY HARD WORKERS. GIVE THEM SOME CHICKEN.

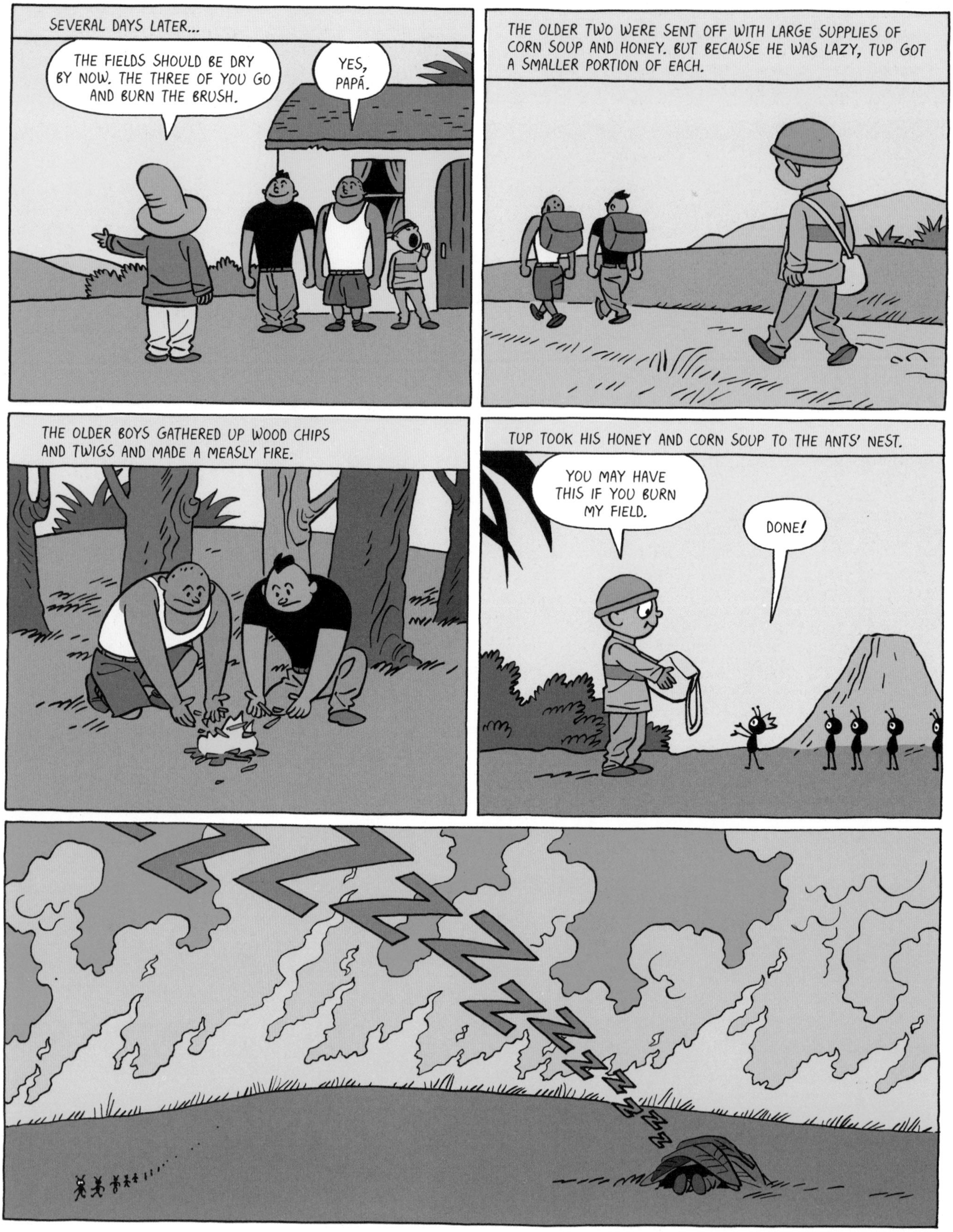
SEVERAL DAYS LATER...
THE FIELDS SHOULD BE DRY BY NOW. THE THREE OF YOU GO AND BURN THE BRUSH.
YES, PAPÁ.
THE OLDER TWO WERE SENT OFF WITH LARGE SUPPLIES OF CORN SOUP AND HONEY. BUT BECAUSE HE WAS LAZY, TUP GOT A SMALLER PORTION OF EACH.
THE OLDER BOYS GATHERED UP WOOD CHIPS AND TWIGS AND MADE A MEASLY FIRE.
TUP TOOK HIS HONEY AND CORN SOUP TO THE ANTS' NEST.
YOU MAY HAVE THIS IF YOU BURN MY FIELD.
DONE!
ZZZZZZZZZZZ

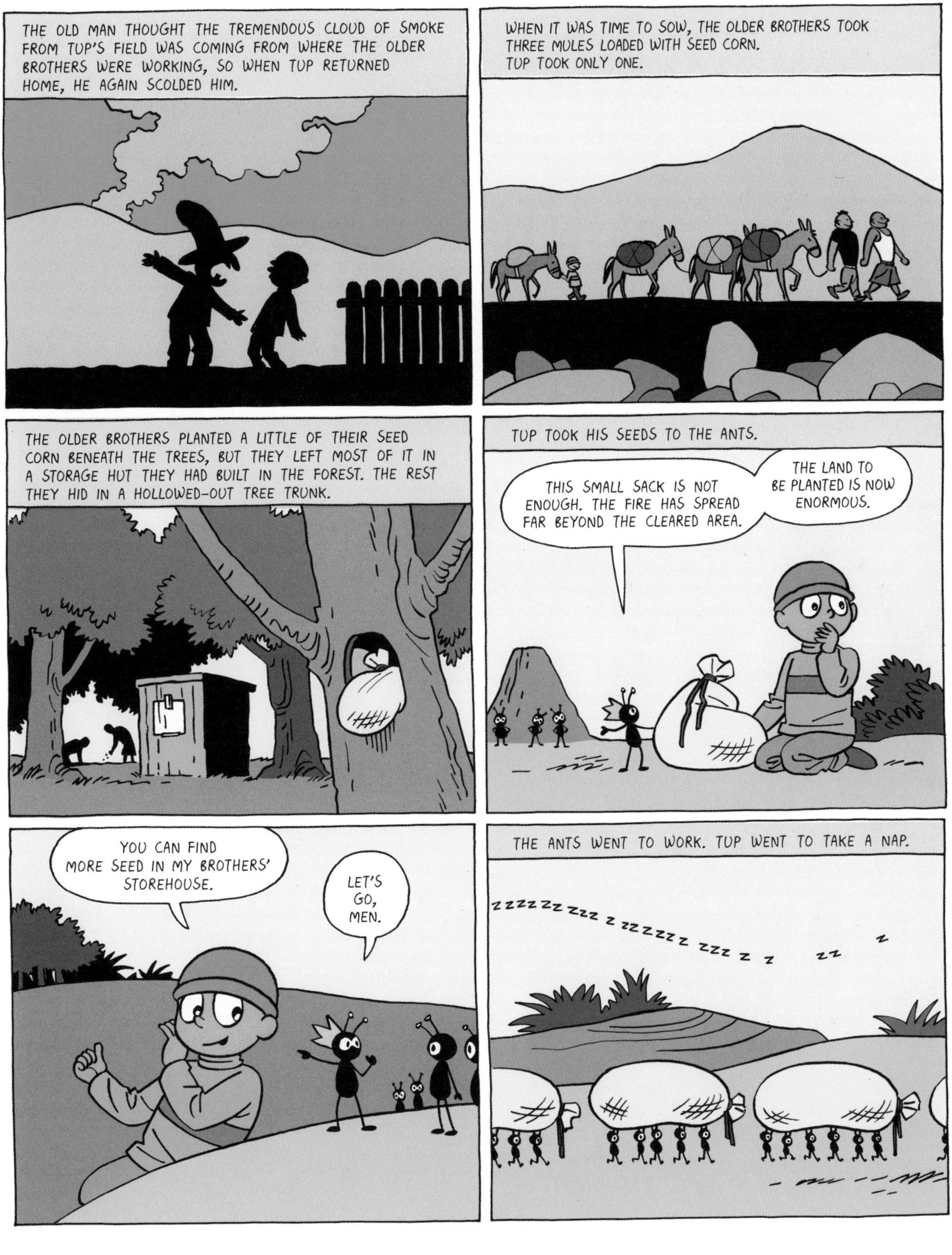

THE OLD MAN THOUGHT THE TREMENDOUS CLOUD OF SMOKE FROM TUP'S FIELD WAS COMING FROM WHERE THE OLDER BROTHERS WERE WORKING, SO WHEN TUP RETURNED HOME, HE AGAIN SCOLDED HIM.
WHEN IT WAS TIME TO SOW, THE OLDER BROTHERS TOOK THREE MULES LOADED WITH SEED CORN. TUP TOOK ONLY ONE.
THE OLDER BROTHERS PLANTED A LITTLE OF THEIR SEED CORN BENEATH THE TREES, BUT THEY LEFT MOST OF IT IN A STORAGE HUT THEY HAD BUILT IN THE FOREST. THE REST THEY HID IN A HOLLOWED-OUT TREE TRUNK.
TUP TOOK HIS SEEDS TO THE ANTS.
THIS SMALL SACK IS NOT ENOUGH. THE FIRE HAS SPREAD FAR BEYOND THE CLEARED AREA.
THE LAND TO BE PLANTED IS NOW ENORMOUS.
YOU CAN FIND MORE SEED IN MY BROTHERS' STOREHOUSE.
LET'S GO, MEN.
THE ANTS WENT TO WORK. TUP WENT TO TAKE A NAP.
ZZZZZZ ZZZ Z ZZZZZZ ZZZ Z Z ZZ Z

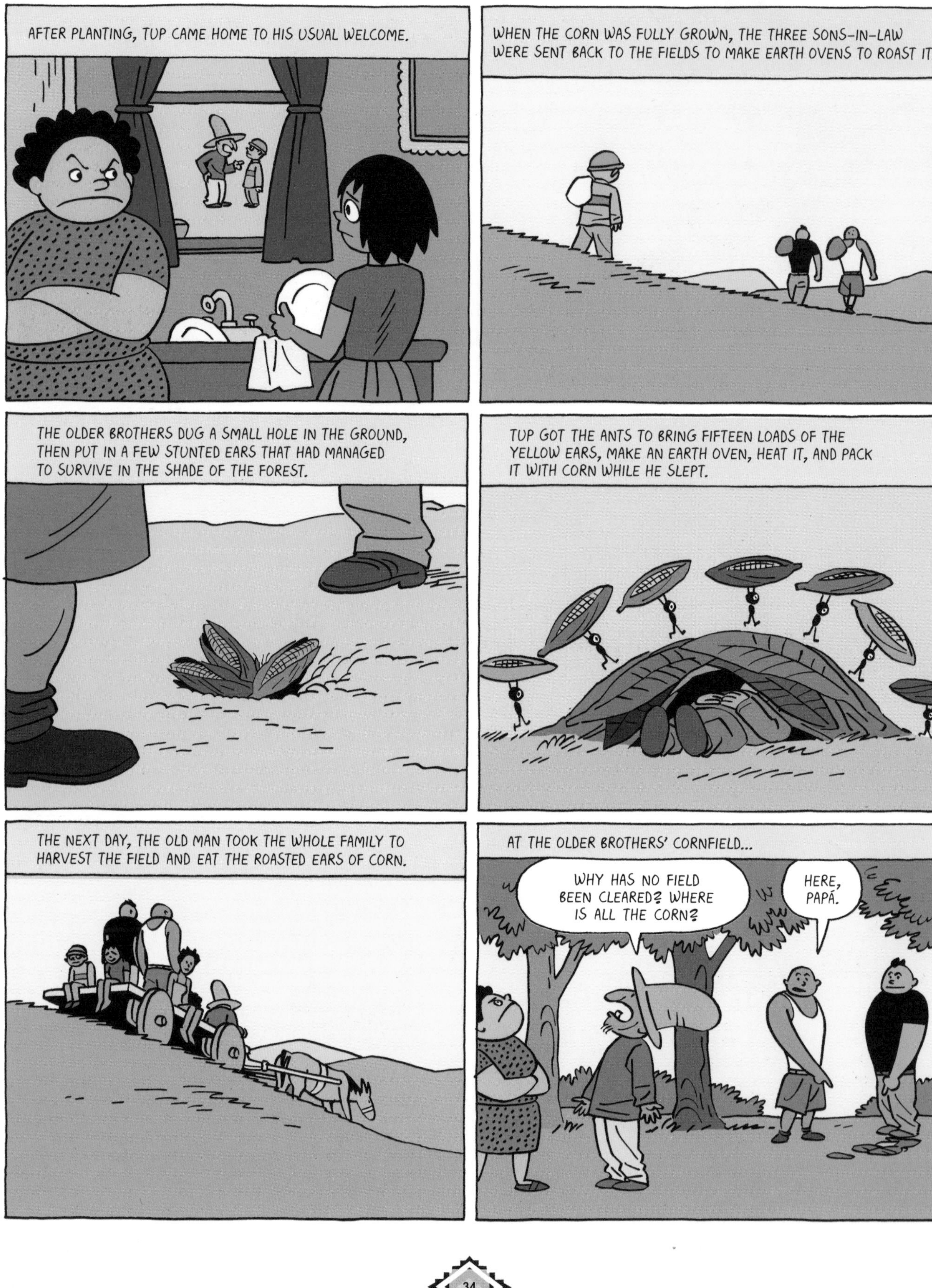
AFTER PLANTING, TUP CAME HOME TO HIS USUAL WELCOME.
WHEN THE CORN WAS FULLY GROWN, THE THREE SONS-IN-LAW WERE SENT BACK TO THE FIELDS TO MAKE EARTH OVENS TO ROAST IT.
THE OLDER BROTHERS DUG A SMALL HOLE IN THE GROUND, THEN PUT IN A FEW STUNTED EARS THAT HAD MANAGED TO SURVIVE IN THE SHADE OF THE FOREST.
TUP GOT THE ANTS TO BRING FIFTEEN LOADS OF THE YELLOW EARS, MAKE AN EARTH OVEN, HEAT IT, AND PACK IT WITH CORN WHILE HE SLEPT.
THE NEXT DAY, THE OLD MAN TOOK THE WHOLE FAMILY TO HARVEST THE FIELD AND EAT THE ROASTED EARS OF CORN.
AT THE OLDER BROTHERS' CORNFIELD...
WHY HAS NO FIELD BEEN CLEARED? WHERE IS ALL THE CORN?
HERE, PAPÁ.

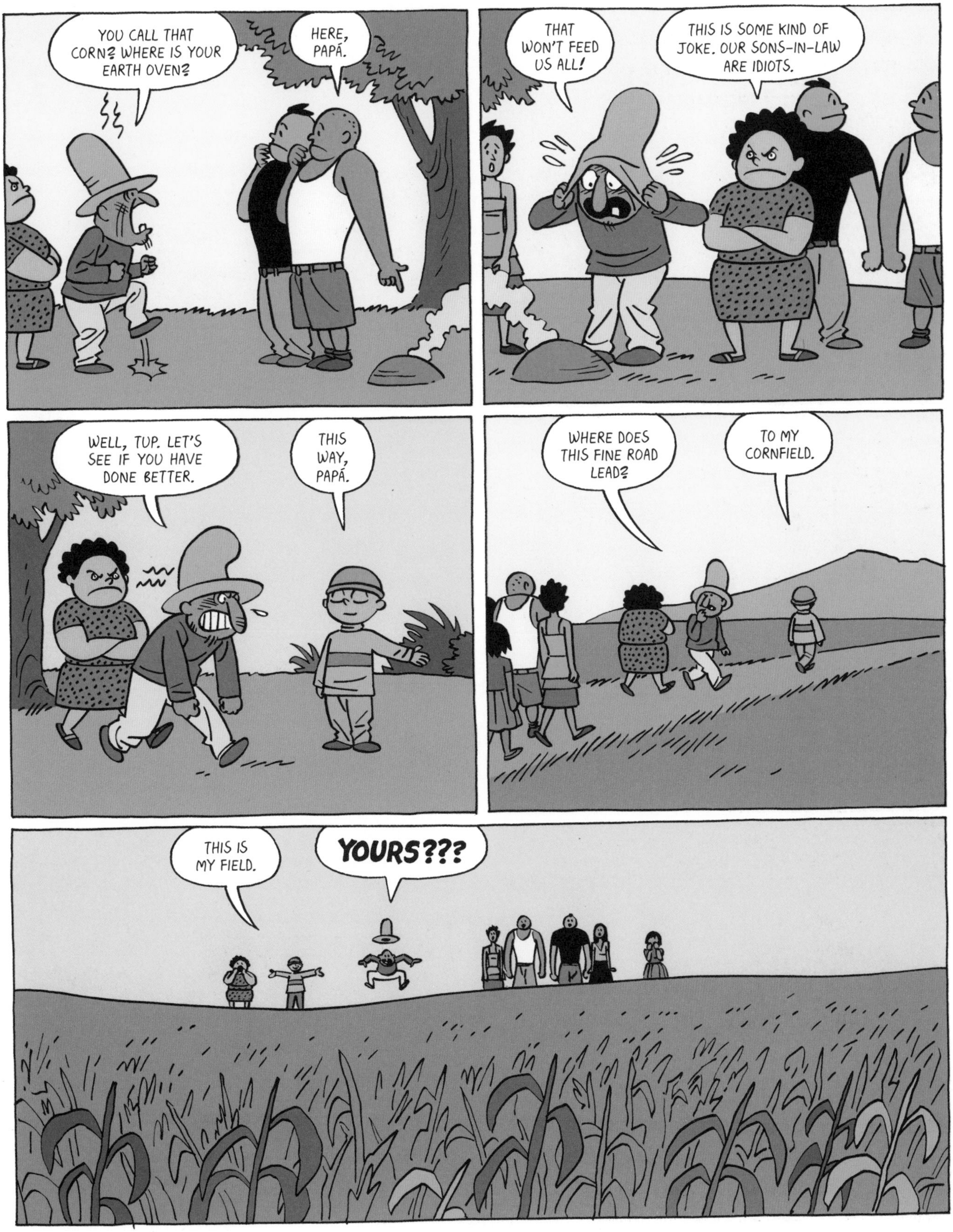
YOU CALL THAT CORN? WHERE IS YOUR EARTH OVEN?
HERE, PAPÁ.
THAT WON'T FEED US ALL!
THIS IS SOME KIND OF JOKE. OUR SONS-IN-LAW ARE IDIOTS.
WELL, TUP. LET'S SEE IF YOU HAVE DONE BETTER.
THIS WAY, PAPÁ.
WHERE DOES THIS FINE ROAD LEAD?
TO MY CORNFIELD.
THIS IS MY FIELD.
YOURS???

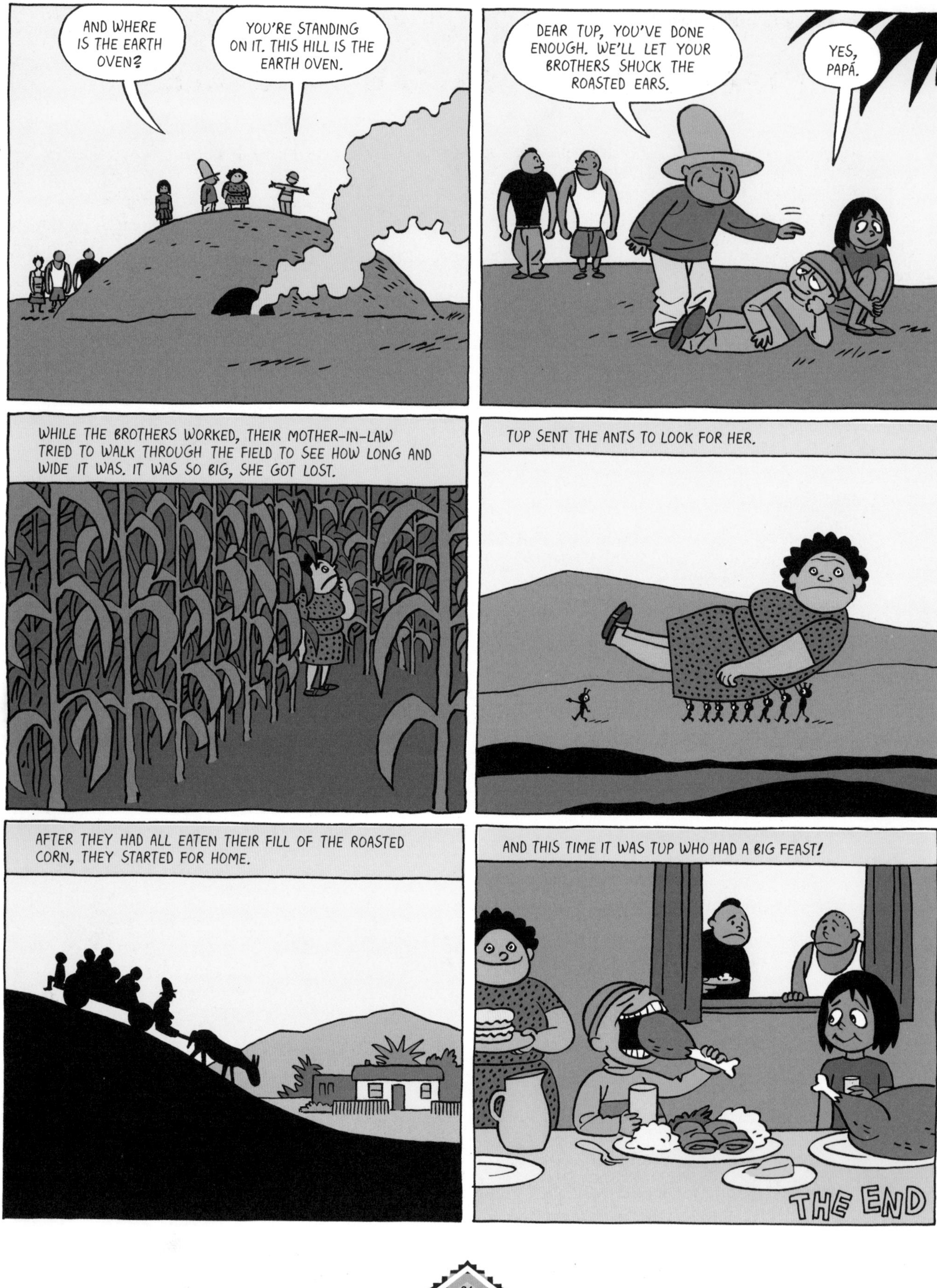
AND WHERE IS THE EARTH OVEN?
YOU'RE STANDING ON IT. THIS HILL IS THE EARTH OVEN.
DEAR TUP, YOU'VE DONE ENOUGH. WE'LL LET YOUR BROTHERS SHUCK THE ROASTED EARS.
YES, PAPÁ.
WHILE THE BROTHERS WORKED, THEIR MOTHER-IN-LAW TRIED TO WALK THROUGH THE FIELD TO SEE HOW LONG AND WIDE IT WAS. IT WAS SO BIG, SHE GOT LOST.
TUP SENT THE ANTS TO LOOK FOR HER.
AFTER THEY HAD ALL EATEN THEIR FILL OF THE ROASTED CORN, THEY STARTED FOR HOME.
AND THIS TIME IT WAS TUP WHO HAD A BIG FEAST!
THE END

THREE LATIN AMERICAN FOLKTALES

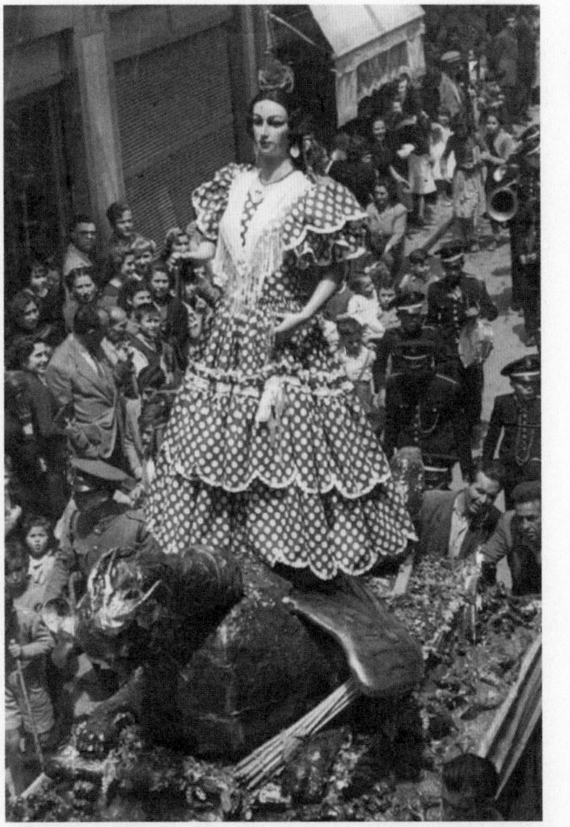

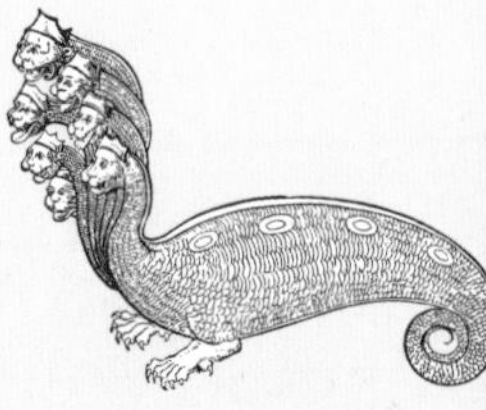

When we tell folktales, we pass on our ideas about history, art, spirituality, and proper behavior to a new generation. And when we hear folktales, we learn about the values and customs of our ancestors. THE DRAGON SLAYER, for example, teaches us how important it is to be generous with those people who seek our help and to resist those who try to harm us. In some versions of this story told throughout the Hispanic and Latino world, the old woman who asks for food is said to be the Virgin Mary, honored by the Catholic Church as the mother of Jesus. The story's religious origins don't stop there: in Spain, *La Tarasca*, a gigantic woman warrior standing over a conquered beast, is paraded each year during the Feast of Corpus Christi. In the southern town of Antequera, La Tarasca is shown having vanquished a dragon with seven heads, one for each of the cardinal sins. While there have been dragon-slaying tales from time immemorial – Hercules, who slew the hydra, or Saint George, the patron saint of England – many feature a man who rescues a damsel in distress. The heroine of THE DRAGON SLAYER shows us how important it is for young women to take charge of their own lives: they might even end up being the ones who save the prince's life.

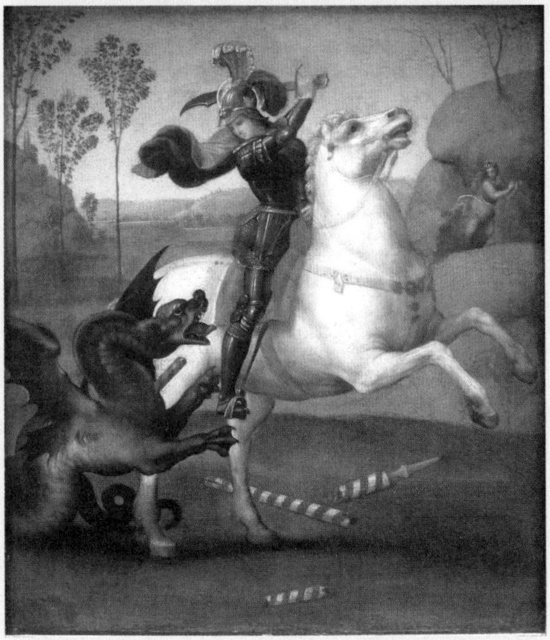

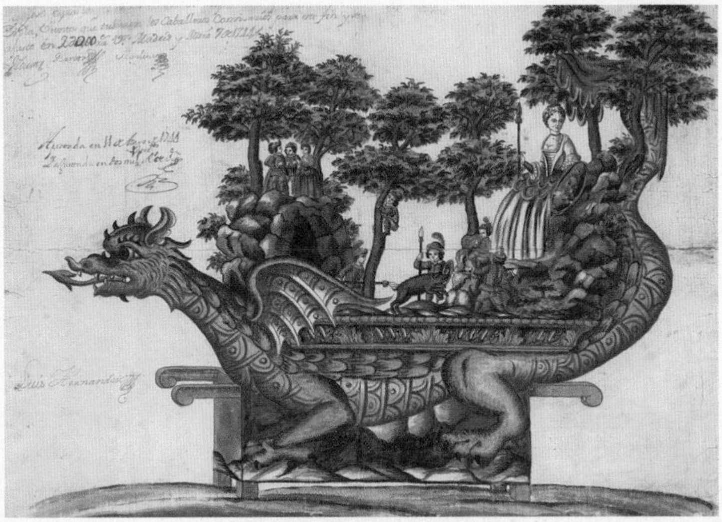

Clockwise from top left: A parade of La Tarasca through the streets in Spain in 1959; engraving of a seven-headed dragon; the Tarasca float in Madrid in 1744; Saint George Conquering the Dragon, *circa 1504, a painting by Raphael at the Musée du Louvre in Paris, France.*

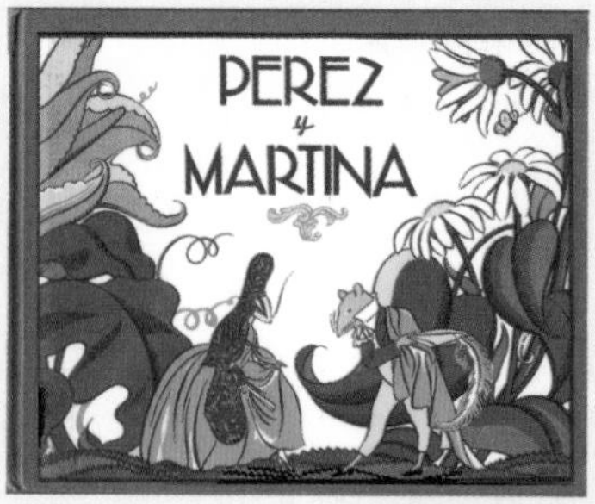
PEREZ
y
MARTINA

Pérez and Martina *by Pura Delpré, 1932, was the first Spanish-language book for children published by a mainstream U.S. press.*

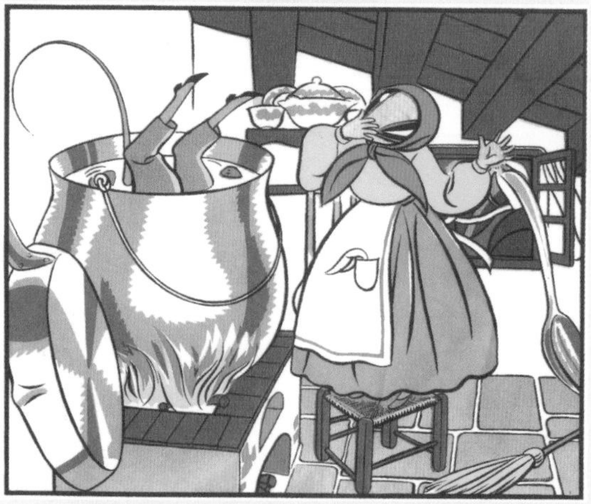

Another example of a female rescuer is Doña Pepa, the woman healer in the tale of MARTINA MARTÍNEZ AND PÉREZ THE MOUSE. She's the only character who knows how to save Pérez from drowning. While this particular version of the tale is written by the children's book author Alma Flor Ada, the story of Ratón Pérez's marriage is one of the most popular and best loved folktales in Hispanic and Latino culture. Different storytellers make Martina into a cockroach, an ant, or a rat. In some versions, Pérez isn't rescued at the end – making this story perfect for sharing at a *velorio*, or wake. The velorio is an all-night meeting of friends and family after someone dies. Tradition holds that if someone falls asleep at the velorio, the soul of the recently departed person will enter his or her body, so everyone in attendance from *abuelas* (grandmothers) to traveling farm workers tells thrilling stories to keep the group awake. Storytellers use gestures, facial expressions, different voices, and many jokes to prevent their audience from dozing off.

Below: El velorio / The Wake *by Francisco Oller, painted in 1893, hangs in the Museum of Anthropology and History of the University of Puerto Rico.*

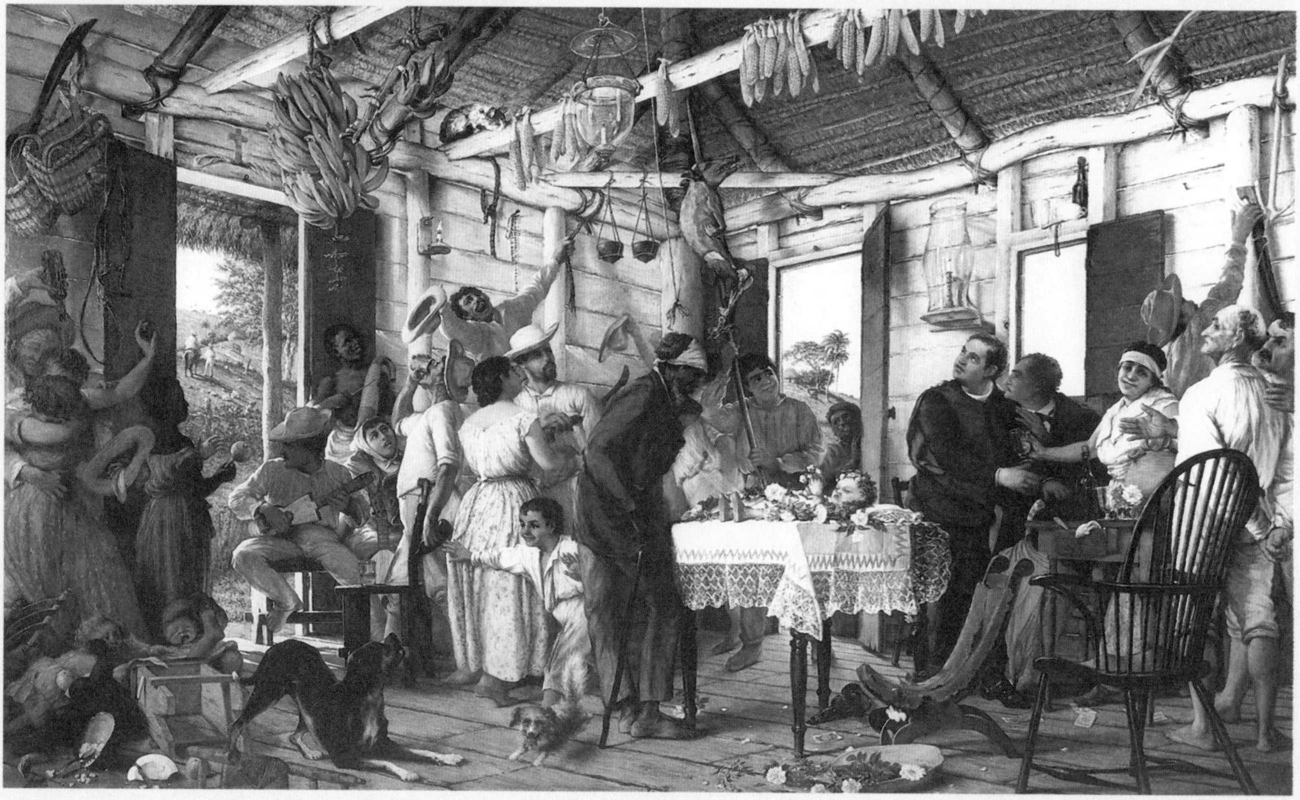

Every popular folktale contains both moral lessons (like the importance of bravery) and practical lessons (like how to behave after a loved one dies). TUP AND THE ANTS teaches both, too: it shows those who hear it the value of cleverness and of not following instructions literally, but it also informs them on how to plant their crops. Tup's story comes from the Yucatán Peninsula in southeastern Mexico, where, in ancient times, crops such as corn and tomatoes were first cultivated. Spanish colonists introduced these and many other fruits and vegetables to the rest of the world, and they are now found almost everywhere. Aztec and Maya farmers used a traditional practice called *milpa* to plant crops. Even today, just like Tup, milpa farmers, or *milperos*, cut down and burn patches of the rain forest in order to create rich, fertile land for growing corn. The farmers also rotate their crops to make sure not to exhaust the soil. This method takes a lot of patience and advance planning – much of it is explained in the story.

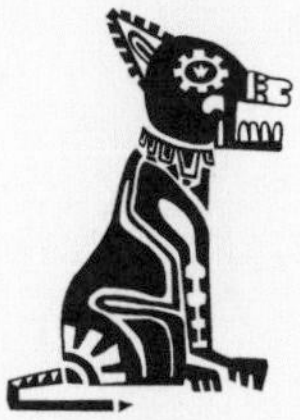

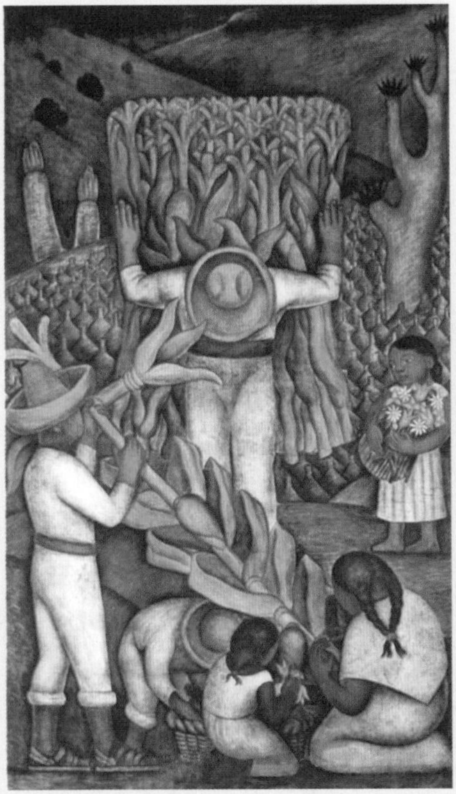

Diego Rivera, a world-renowned Mexican painter, depicted the tools and techniques of local methods of agriculture in many murals.

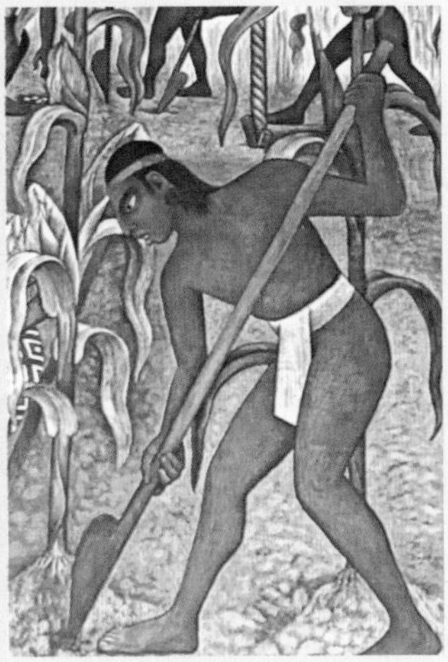

TELL YOUR OWN STORY

It is part of the oral tradition for the performer to embroider the tale and make it his or her own. Storytellers like to use stock phrases to capture their audience's attention when they start and end their stories. Here are some of them, in Spanish and English:

¿Quieres que te cuente un cuento?
Do you want to hear a story?

Había una vez.../ Érase una vez...
Once upon a time...

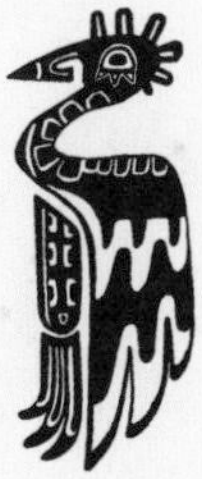

Hace mucho tiempo...
A long time ago...

Cuentan que...
The story goes that...

En un país muy lejano...
In a far-off land...

En la tierra del olvido, donde de nada nadie se acuerda, había...
In the land where all is forgotten, where no one remembers anything, there was...

...y colorín colorado, este cuento se ha acabado.
...and so, my fine-feathered friend, now the story has found an end.

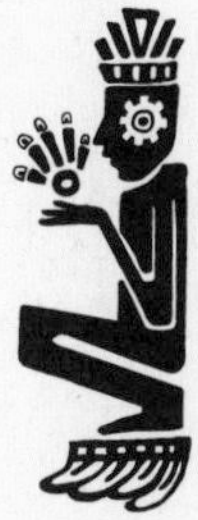

...y vivieron felices para siempre.
...and everyone lived happily ever after.

From *Tales Our Abuelitas Told*, by F. Isabel Campoy and Alma Flor Ada

Tup, Martina Martínez, Ratón Pérez, and the dragon slayer all give us different lessons from the past and show us how to prepare for the future. The details of their stories may change from storyteller to storyteller, but the values they reflect – from faith to love to loyalty – are timeless.

ABOUT THE AUTHORS

JAIME HERNANDEZ is the co-creator, along with his brothers Gilbert and Mario, of the comic book series *Love and Rockets*. Since publishing the first issue of *Love and Rockets* in 1981, Jaime has won an Eisner Award, 12 Harvey Awards, and the Los Angeles Times Book Prize. The *New York Times Book Review* calls him "one of the most talented artists our polyglot culture has ever produced." Jaime decided to create THE DRAGON SLAYER, his first book for young readers, because "I thought it would be a nice change of pace from my usual grown-up comics." He read through tons of folktales to choose these three. What made them stand out? Maybe he saw himself in their characters. Jaime says, "I'm not as brave as the dragon slayer, but I can be as caring. I'm as lazy as Tup without being as resourceful. I am not as vain as Martina, but I can be as foolish."

F. ISABEL CAMPOY and **ALMA FLOR ADA** are authors of many award-winning children's books, including *Tales Our Abuelitas Told*, a collection of Hispanic folktales that includes MARTINA MARTÍNEZ AND PÉREZ THE MOUSE. Alma Flor says, "My favorite moment in the story is when Ratón Pérez is pulled out of the pot of soup!" As scholars devoted to the study of language and literacy, Alma Flor and Isabel love to share Hispanic and Latino culture with young readers. "Folktales are a valuable heritage we have received from the past, and we must treasure them and pass them along," Isabel says. "If you do not have roots, you will not have fruits."

BIBLIOGRAPHY

Tales Our Abuelitas Told: A Hispanic Folktale Collection, F. Isabel Campoy and Alma Flor Ada (Authors), Atheneum Books for Young Readers, 2006. *Twelve stories from varied roots of Hispanic culture. Ages 5-10*

———

Latin American Folktales: Stories from the Hispanic and Indian Tradition, John Bierhorst, Pantheon Books, 2002. *A collection of Latin American stories sourced from twenty countries.*

The Monkey's Haircut and Other Stories Told by the Maya, John Bierhorst and Robert Andrew Parker (Illustrator), William Morrow and Company, 1986. *A collection of twenty-two traditional Mayan tales.*

Fiesta Femenina: Celebrating Women in Mexican Folktales, Mary-Joan Gerson, Barefoot Books, 2001. *Eight stories of extraordinary women in Mexican folklore. Ages 8+*

Mexican-American Folklore, John O. West, August House, 2005. *A range of traditional Mexican-American proverbs, riddles, stories and folk songs.*

———

The Day It Snowed Tortillas / El Día Que Nevaron Tortillas: Folktales told in Spanish and English, Joe Hayes & Antonio Castro Lopez, Cinco Puntos Press, 2003. *A collection of New Mexican magical folktales for a modern audience. Ages 10-12*

———

Horse Hooves and Chicken Feet: Mexican Folktales, Neil Philip (Compiler) & Jacqueline Mair (Illustrator), Clarion Books, 2003. *Fifteen classic Mexican folktales. Ages 5-8*

———

Mango, Abuela, and Me, Meg Medina (Author) & Angela Dominguez (Illustrator), Candlewick, 2015. *A girl and her abuela transcend language barriers. Ages 5-8*

Online Resources:

WWW.AMERICANFOLKLORE.NET *Retellings of folktales, myths, legends, fairy tales, superstitions, weather lore, and ghost stories from all over the Americas.*

———

WWW.SURLALUNEFAIRYTALES.COM *Sur La Lune offers over 40 eBooks, including fairy tale and folklore anthologies, critical texts, poetry and fiction.*

———

WWW.STORIESTOGROWBY.ORG *Folk & fairy tales from around the world.*

———

WWW.PITT.EDU/~DASH/FOLKTEXTS.HTML *Offers a variety of folklore and mythology texts, arranged in groups of closely related stories.*

HTTP://ONLINEBOOKS.LIBRARY.UPENN.EDU/ *An index of over two million books readable for free. (Search for subject: tales.)*